UNIVERSITY GOSSIP

by
Brian
Herman

UNIVERSITY GOSSIP

Brian Herman

University Gossip

print ISBN: 978-1-66784-599-9
ebook ISBN: 978-1-66784-600-2

Books by Brian Herman

Short Novels

One Rainy Season in Yunnan: The Path Past Pomasha

University Gossip

Part One

One

From the horizon the sun sent a golden trail shimmering across Pacific waters and onto Panther Beach, where the bright reflection at last settled itself onto the steep shore for evening. Jade and turquoise fingers rustled into seafoam, erasing the memory of the sun from the sand in crashing, forceful cadence.

The marine layer had not yet begun its advance; it still lurked far out above the water, nestled beneath the sun, preparing for its evening offensive. Soon the clouds would creep across Highway 1, past the tidy rows of faculty bungalows, past the palms of the arboretum and up the university drive. This was the last of the golden-hour sunlight. It dripped from the swooping branches of the redwoods and onto the front steps of the Susan E. Gephardt College Apartments.

〜

Under such ideal conditions even the monolithic façade of the apartment block seemed at home among the two and three-story *colleges* dotting the surrounding forest. Not everything had gone according to plan in the construction of the university, and campus housing once consisting of idiosyncratically-designed, community-minded structures had gradually given way to a landscape of monotonous, high-rise apartments.

Within one such structure, two sophomores on a balcony, each in a plastic chair, examples of countless fellow sophomores exiled to the Gephardt College Apartments, ventured into their usual state of affairs:

"Weiwei Li threw up all over herself last night," announced MacKenzie Benoit. "I'm not sure why she keeps doing that to herself over Payton Carruthers. He's *sooo* not worth it."

MacKenzie's glass of rosé sat waiting, only momentarily forgotten, propped in her hand by freshly painted fingers. With the other hand, she pointed to her glass and asked, "Zora, darling, would you pour me a little more?" Then, without the slightest hint of irony, MacKenzie Benoit cheered: "Box wine is the best! Isn't it the best? I absolutely *L-O-V-E, love*, box wine!"

"Who doesn't love box wine?" Agreed Zora, the more reticent of the two young women. "Box wine and Black Cherry White Claw, that's all I need to survive."

"White Claw! *Umm*, really? That's so *fire*. You like Black Cherry?"

"Yes, honey."

"Wow, I thought Mango was everyone's favorite White Claw."

"Mango's for white girls, honey."

"Oh, wow, *like*, I never knew that."

MacKenzie Benoit considered the effects flavor names might play on diverse sets of consumer groups. Soon enough though, this brief thought faded into the same languid sort of submission that most undergraduate students find unavoidable on warm autumn evenings.

MacKenzie's was a bright, crisp face, the kind one might have expected to see in a gloooy, teen magazine, when publications were still read in that format. Her skin was milky white without powder, and her cheek bones still bore wildly at times, the natural rouge of youth. The hair was *the hair*—it was the envy of MacKenzie's contemporaries and what women of all ages suggested first when prompted to describe MacKenzie's appearance. Her hair was long, mahogany and lustrous—and it helped—fortunately for MacKenzie—to balance out her rather large nose. This, it must be said, was the sort of appendage a well-heeled woman would eventually need to sort out with the right type of surgeon; but for now, such an idea was only a kernel in the recesses of MacKenzie's greatest desires, to be fleshed out later in womanhood, when the freedom of age and her own, earned money would permit. Even so, she still hovered on the attractive side. This was made all the more obvious in the way she pursed her lips—in a manner giving casual viewers the impression that Ms. Benoit was savoring a single, melting Jordan almond.

~

"I think I hear *Double Wei* in there now," Zora Weaver shrugged toward the sliding glass door.

"*What*?" asked MacKenzie, never quite disengaging from the communication device in her lap, and more to indicate indifference rather than not having heard.

"*I said* I think I hear Weiwei Li in there now," repeated the more reticent of the two as she tipped curls toward the sliding glass door.

And then presently the head of Weiwei Li did indeed appear in the doorway. "MacKenzie! Zora! My girls!!! Box Wine! I love box wine! Let me go get a glass!"

∾

Just as quickly as it had appeared, the excited, if not ill-proportioned, head of Weiwei Li once again disappeared into the cool, musty darkness of the apartment.

Zora Weaver tipped her head again toward the sliding glass door, casually aware of the full glass of wine balancing atop her right thigh. She asked, "Do you think she heard us talking?"

The corners of MacKenzie's mouth had only just turned down, and in the time it had taken to express this insouciance, Weiwei Li had returned to the balcony with a wine glass.

Two

Weiwei Li wore a fast-fashion sweatsuit and a NY Yankees baseball cap set at an off-angle. *The sweatsuit was Weiwei's constant attire* around the apartment suite, and the extent to which Weiwei remained in uniform, as it were, often led the other girls to speculate on the state of its cleanliness. Weiwei was a little on the plump side, probably more bloated from White Claw and free fraternity party beer than for any other reason. She was what the other Health and Wellness girls would politely describe as *"not fully aware of her body,"* or, much worse, *"not completely focused on her health."*

After a freshman year spent trying to seduce boys into saying *and really believing* she was sexy, Weiwei had lowered her ambitions. She wished now only to be seen as *quirky,* or even *cute*—if that's what it had to be—and she had recently begun listening to the anime show on the campus radio station in an attempt to bolster these efforts.

"I'm so glad I ran into you," effused an excitable Weiwei. "It's so weird, but sometimes it's ages before we actually see each other in this place. As Health and Wellness girls we share a common bond—so that means we need to get together more often for box wine!"

Then, when the other two remained completely silent: "It's just so nice to see you!"

"I know, right?" Offered MacKenzie, mostly to avoid another uncomfortable silence. "I feel so lucky Zora and I got paired with you and LaLa in the housing lottery. Our Bigs always know what's best—and we *do* need to hang out more. Cheers to that."

"MacKenzie, remember last year when you lived down the hall from me in Slater Quad?" Weiwei asked rhetorically. "That was before we even joined Health and Wellness. *Omigod*, if it weren't for you, I wouldn't have ever known about the activities fair or about *any* of this. I am *soo* glad we aren't in Slater anymore. It's so much nicer having a drink here on our own balcony, even if it is a little far away from everything."

~

Just across the university drive, nearly a year before, MacKenzie's ground floor, corner room had been the social hub of Slater Hall. There, a one-year milkier and more pouting MacKenzie Benoit held court on domestic matters both straight-forward and not, confident in her role as dormitory sage from four long winters spent at a Connecticut preparatory academy. Nevertheless, as freshman year cliques forced into formation by geographic proximity and organized identity-building gave way to the boundary-expanding metamorphoses of that fresh-man spring, MacKenzie had quite consciously drifted away from her freshman-year circle of friends. Her sway over the girls from down the hall, to the enduring credit of MacKenzie's well-honed social awareness, remained, or was even strengthened by her revised demeanor and cooler attitude toward her dormitory neighbors.

MacKenzie's invitation to join the Health and Wellness house had been a personal one; it came from the chair of the recruitment committee herself. It was only in a moment of misguided weakness that MacKenzie had foolishly mentioned her plans to visit the Health and Wellness table at the activities fair to the dormitory set. This mistake had since become the greatest regret of MacKenzie's young life. Even so, there was still a glimmer of the same courtesy which had served as currency in the formation of the girls' relationship one year earlier.

"How are things on the Board of Directors?" Weiwei asked.

"Horrible. Scheduling out the studio is driving us all insane."

"Bikram and Kundalini?"

"No, not this time. Pilates and Mindful Meditation."

"*Ah.*"

"The Mindful Meditation series has been a particular problem. For some reason, and I'll never know why, the Bigs *love* Emma Swain. If Emma proposes something, *anything,* then it's always a good idea. It literally makes me want to vomit. *So*—Emma proposes doing Mindful Meditation on Tuesdays and Thursdays from five-thirty to seven-thirty. But this time has always been reserved for Kayla Arroyo's Pilates class. *I love*

that Pilates class, *L-O-V-E, love,* and poor Kayla, getting forced ·
out of her slot like that. Who wants to just sit around hum-
ming and breathing in all that nasty incense at five-thirty on a
Tuesday evening? Not me. I need to sweat. So there is going to
be a Board of Directors vote to decide.

"The Board is leaning toward Emma, of course. I think it's
gonna be a close vote due to a number of factors. For example,
I heard that Kayla Arroyo made out with Caden Dunwoody
at a party recently, and this was while Caden was still dating
one of the Bigs—I don't really want to say who—but *ehh-nee-
way*—I'm not saying that something like that *would* affect the
vote, but it certainly *could.* The Board of Directors always has
trouble deciding these sorts of matters. The Bigs don't know
anything about *our* year, and with eight Bigs on the Board and
only me to represent our class, who knows how it's going to
work out. If Kayla loses her yoga time, then she'll also lose her
title as Wellness Officer. This is ever since the Bigs made that
silly rule about Wellness Officers having to serve double-duty
as yoga leads. I would totally be a Wellness Officer if I weren't
already on the Board, and if I were a Wellness Officer, I would
keep Pilates at five-thirty on Tuesdays and Thursdays no matter what.

"The Pilates class was the first one I ever took at Health
and Wellness. That was last year when we were all rushing. *I
love Pilates!* I would totally go to Pilates every day if we had
it. Kayla would have probably been able to keep her slot if it
weren't for the thing about Caden Dunwoody, but now I'm
not sure. *I like Kayla.* She does a really good job at working

with what she has. Her legs aren't really the type that the swimmers or football players go for, they're a little stumpy—and she has that thing with her teeth—but some boys do still seem to like her.

"The lone consolation about any of this, from my perspective, is that since Mindful Meditation doesn't count as yoga, Emma Swain must not be planning to take over Kayla's Wellness Officer position. Why she's doing it then—I have no clue. *It doesn't make any sense to me,* but I guess that crazy girl just really loves to meditate.

"*But poor Kayla.* Potentially losing your Wellness Officer role for no reason. It's undignified and absolutely ridiculous. No wonder she's lashing out and kissing everyone's boyfriends at the water polo house when she gets drunk. The water polo house is the place to go get drunk and make out with other people's boyfriends. *Everybody knows that.* So I say we should just be supportive of *her journey,* no matter where that *journey* leads her." MacKenzie kicked back a formidable gulp of wine. "I don't really know how the Board will react if Kayla loses her title. I'm not sure we've ever been put in this position before."

～

Were this discourse directed at any of the other Health and Wellness girls and not Weiwei Li, their interest would have much sooner succumbed to alternate, competing thoughts of greater or lesser importance. Weiwei's attention, however, remained transfixed.

"I've always wondered what it might be like to be a Wellness Officer," she began the detailed pitch for which she had prepared in advance. "I've been taking yoga ever since I joined Health and Wellness, and now I think I'm ready to teach. Plus, I also think my being a Liberal Education major would help when we initiate the pledges."

Weiwei continued her expression of interest while MacKenzie flung oblique glances across the balcony at Zora Weaver, who busied herself in refilling the glasses when their contents began to run low. It was in this manner that the conversation progressed for the better part of a quarter hour, with Weiwei Li laying forth her merits for candidacy, and MacKenzie, well in line with the custom of the time and the place, doing her best to refrain from listening.

Three

The manner in which the softening of the light brought with it the cool, briny air of evening engendered within even MacKenzie Benoit the possibility of self-reflection. Amidst her well-trained—if not genuine—enrapturement in Weiwei's monologue, MacKenzie returned to the perfectly hung Christmas lights of Greenwich; to spirited lobster bakes in the Hamptons; to Lin-Manuel Miranda rapping at the Richard Rogers Theatre; to meeting her father in the summers for lunches of pumpkin ravioli "at the Club"; eleven philistine football players serenading on the front stoop the night before the Homecoming Game; her younger sister's dance academy recitals; untold trophies and innumerable certificates and clippings to signify the proper level of drive.

Weiwei's past was more mundane. Her parents owned a dry-cleaning business in a strip mall in Woodland Hills. They had saved and borrowed to send Weiwei and her sisters to university. Weiwei hoped for an opportunity that might one day open the door to her own garden of earthly delights.

Thankfully for everyone in attendance on the balcony, Weiwei eventually decided to interrupt herself to announce:

"Like, I should probably be going now. *Issues in Educational Reform* starts in half an hour and I'm totally gross."

But instead of leaving just then, Weiwei got up and leisurely poured herself another half glass. She turned to face her suitemates and asked: "Well, what do you think? If Kayla loses her position, do you think I should try to go out for Wellness Officer? Or would Kayla hate me? You always seem to be so in tune with what's going on, Zora. What do *you* think?"

"*Oh,* that would never work," MacKenzie interjected, unfalteringly ready with an appropriate response. "This much has already been discussed by the Board, and with social justice and equity being at the forefront of everything we do at Health and Wellness these days, it's obvious to everyone that we need to fill a position vacated by an underrepresented minority with another individual of similar background. Don't you agree, Zora?"

When the reserved young woman on the other side of the balcony offered nothing in reply, MacKenzie continued:

"Everyone needs to do their part to ensure social equity. *I'm so sorry, Weiwei.* As Health and Wellness girls we're all responsible for the optics of our organizational structure.

"It is each of our own responsibilities, in fact, to promote social equity, and probably more important to our collective future than either health or wellness. Before Kayla, none of the members of the Board or in a Wellness Officer position was a minority. I mean, sure, we had Christina Park on the Board and Misaki Saito-Jones in place as a Wellness Officer, but let's be honest, most Asians are just as bad as white for what

I'm talking about. Unfortunately, we are only now as a society unburying ourselves from this awkward history. All twenty of the founders of Health and Wellness House were white girls from Slater Quad. Well, maybe there was one Asian—*but whatever*—you get my point. We all share the responsibility of righting these wrongs, and because of that, we can't always get things the way we want.

"I actually don't think we'll be able to appoint anyone who isn't an underrepresented minority to *any* position for some time. All of the other houses on campus are in the same position as us, except the ones that are entirely made up of minorities already. They had a head start on us *for sure*.

"I heard that last year, when Kayla Arroyo was first going out for the Wellness Officer position, Hannah Morgan wanted it too. You know, *Guru Hannah Morgan*. I mean Hannah spent a month during her gap year at an ashram in Uttar Pradesh eating only lentils and yoghurt. I don't know if the two of you ever knew that—but that's why her pledge name was *Guru*. So Hannah Morgan was qualified and maybe even *more* qualified than Kayla Arroyo for the role, but the Bigs, in their ultimate wisdom, knew we had to enhance our diversity profile. This was my first or second month on the Board, and the Bigs asked me to talk to Hannah about it, since she's in our class. Everything turned out ok in the end; she took it well. I think we found her something to do on the social committee for a semester until she started teaching Vinyasa at the University Fitness Center, part-time. We weren't as familiar with these issues then, but now, thank God, it's more or less understood. Hannah Morgan was always a little too beans and seeds for me anyway. I always appreciated Kayla's energy level and understated style, and I didn't think she ever spent too much time lingering on the silly, meditative parts of yoga."

Then MacKenzie sent a poison dart through Weiwei's wounded heart: "One thing we *were* thinking about is that *Zora* might be interested in running for the open Wellness Officer position. Isn't that right, Zora?" MacKenzie gave precious little time for a response before adding, "It's just what is right for the times, I guess.

"Now, of course, Weiwei, you're certainly free to do anything you want. We Health and Wellness girls must always stick to our principles. Look at Hannah, she stuck to it and now she even has a paid work-study gig at the University Fitness Center. That Hannah Morgan has something figured out, I have to hand it to her, even in spite of the beans and the seeds, I have to admit."

"I'm sorry I've taken up so much of your time," Weiwei uttered meekly as she got up to leave. She staggered a few paces on the balcony like a wounded fawn. "The Wellness Officer position is obviously not the right fit for me. And now here *Issues in Educational Reform* is about to start and I'm still so gross. I can't wait to see you both at Kundalini on Sunday. I'm sure I'll be able to find something else to do, *somewhere*. Anyway, I have to get going. I totally need to shower before class."

Then Weiwei, in her fast-fashion sweatsuit, limped away.

~

It was dusk now. Perambulating students trod the worn paths through the redwoods on their way to evening classes. Bicyclists found the shortest routes as they pedaled and huffed up the university drive toward the student union.

"How do you think she took it?" Asked Zara Weaver

"She's a doll. She understands."

"Do you think somebody told her about it all being fixed?"

"I'm sure she must've heard something. She's been dropping hints, *you know,* about wanting to be a Wellness Officer, for absolutely forever. No one on the Board was ever much good at keeping secrets anyway. But the end result is that we'll have our first ever black Wellness Officer and she will be you. *Yay!* Hey, by the way, don't you have *Fundamentals of Nonprofit Organizations* tonight?"

"No—I mean—*yes, sort-of.* I'm starting my *Fundamentals of Nonprofits* internship at the Soldiers' Memorial Services Center tonight. They've asked me to stop by to help with a seminar before my first real shift next week. The Soldiers' Memorial Services Center is *such* a better assignment than Juvenile Hall or patient navigation at the hospital. Do you want to come along with me to see?"

"No, darling, of course not. I'm afraid that other than keeping the girls of Health and Wellness in fabulous shape and on the right side of the rules, I'm not much for supporting the community at large. I don't enjoy seeing people with messy hair and hairy moles and food stuck in their beards. Last spring, when we collected canned goods for the Second Chance Center, I could barely bring myself to go inside. That smell was just horrible. No Zora, that's why I'm a finance major. There's no need for me to care about anyone other than *me and my girls*. But I will say, I do donate my old *J Crew* every year, and this year I also donated some *Vineyard Vines*. I'm sure we'll all be forced to go to another horrible service project sometime eventually anyway—probably this spring. I'll leave it to you, my dear, to save the world one person at a time.

"Did you ever see the play *Peter Pan* online when you were young? When I was a kid one of my nannies was *this* middle-aged spinster from down the street who was obsessed with it. Anyway, what happens is that a little flying boy comes to the nursery window to whisk a girl and her younger brothers away to Neverland. I could never understand why the girl wanted to go and sleep in a cardboard box in the forest and tussle with pirates and Indians all day. I always thought there must have been something wrong with her. She already lived in a luxurious flat in London and had everything she ever needed. That's what you and everyone in the liberal studies programs are to me. You are the little children who go along to Neverland to spend all your time with the people who never shower."

Now MacKenzie was on a roll:

"I knew a family in Greenwich who had a little Bichon Frise named Upsy—you know—like *Upsy-Daisey*. I never quite got that, but people in Greenwich are *weird*. Anyway they loved poor Upsy so much that they kept her alive well after it would have been merciful to put her down. When Upsy's teeth fell out they took her to ultrasonic mouth cleaning appointments every week. When she started peeing everywhere in the house—including on the Persian rugs—they took her to doggie dialysis. Soon the poor little dog was blind and bumping into everything and absolutely miserable. Keeping Upsy alive had nothing to do with Upsy, of course, and everything to do with the owners themselves. A liberal education is like that family was. It's just a way for middle class people to purge their self-indulgent guilt.

"To be honest, Zora, I'm just glad you're starting to take control of some things around here. You deserve it, girl. I'm proud of you! *There*, I can tell you that *at least*, but I wouldn't dare tell you not to waste your time with all those ridiculous service projects you so treasure."

"You always tell me that!"

"*You bitch!* No, I don't. Well, maybe sometimes at parties when the boys are dull and I've had too many White Claws. But never more than once or twice, I'm sure. You're so sharp, Zora. I think I remember recommending you switch majors to Finance or Biological Sciences or something more beneficial. You could always still minor in sweeping up used heroin needles or changing retirees' diapers if you wanted. Where is this services center anyway?"

"It's downtown. They told me to come to the side door on Front Street. Tonight is the first session of a new series. I'm supposed to help take attendance and pass out course materials. Then they said I can stick around and watch the presentation."

"Well, go if you have to. *Save the world.* I'll be here drinking the last of this box wine."

Four

ora took the bus to the edge of campus, then walked past the mission and by the neon bank branches. Inside the Soldiers' Memorial Services Center, a woman at the reception desk was answering an ancient phone:

"Soldiers' Memorial Services Center. *Party please?* Yes, thank you. Please hold."

"Soldiers' Memorial Services Center. *Party please?* Yes, thank you. Please hold."

"Which way to the appreciative inquiry group session?" Zora asked.

The woman pointed brusquely in the direction of a narrow hallway baking under the awkward din of harsh fluorescent lighting. The entire hallway was adorned with portraits of war heroes. Some were painted in oil with unfortunately hasty brushwork; further down, the medium switched to black and white photographs. Irrespective of form, the art was hung in no set pattern, wherever the space between the door jams and the window moulding would allow. A large, solitary Philodendron climbed the wall near the windows, its branches and leaves threatening to displace the clusters of miniature flags and framed group shots of dignitaries lining the window sills. At the end of this distinguished exhibition, there was a free-standing placard in the shape of an arrow which pointed into a well-lit lecture hall. The sign read: *"Appreciative Inquiry Workshop."*

.∩ʋ'

Zora found her way into the room as directed by the arrow and sat in the last of several rows of folding chairs only a few steps from the door. On the table next to her sat blank name tags, markers, a carafe of coffee and a bowl of hard candies. The smell of the building was something akin to a basement annex in a Parish church; crumbled ancient crackers and dust from between the cracks lay unexpurgated by the aroma of the freshly brewing coffee.

Zora drew a small book of philosophy from her purse. Being raised in Berkeley had rendered her pores open for this activity as a regular endeavor; but by now, the compulsion to read and reread often manifested itself at inopportune times. Sometimes the transitory occurrences of the present drifted right past Zora as she hungrily devoured the meanings found inside her favorite works.

∾

Beyond the window stiles, the last remaining tourists of the season trickled out from the bookstore. They dawdled in groups as they decided where to walk for a savory evening meal or a sweet dessert. Zora opened her book to no set page.

She allowed her eyes to rest until they found a manageable portion of familiar text.

"This is the process," she began to read, *"by which through clarity and focus, one may discover the undifferentiated aesthetic continuum as it exists within the mind."* A related sequence of words jumped unexpectedly to her lips, and she corrected herself: *"as it exists within the mind—and without."* Then a sequence of words from a previous page seemed right: *"Draw back the curtain that I may experience the undifferentiated nature of the aesthetic continuum."* She repeated: *"Draw back the curtain that I may experience the undifferentiated aesthetic continuum within myself."*

～

There was a man speaking at the front of the room. The tone of his voice drew Zora from her reverie. It was a nasal, professorial voice, one imbued with a certain wispiness that allowed it to float effortlessly into the rafters, then powerfully all the way to the back of the room:

"With our words, we aim to reinforce more than only the corrective. With our actions, we focus on positive observation and behavior. When you choose to deliver your feedback, no matter the setting, it's important to pay attention to the emotion behind your partner's expression. This is primarily so you can pause long enough to show you are expressing the appropriate amount of empathy."

He continued:

"You see, what we're really getting at here is discussing specific, set ways of speaking to one another to communicate our ideas. And indeed, sometimes we find ourselves asking sensitive questions followed by long, painful silences. Don't be ashamed to wait. We are working on effectively expressing our empathy and love. It can be hard to connect with some people sometimes."

Zora closed and opened her book again: *"Draw back the curtain. Draw back the curtain that I may see—"*

"Modern innovations in technology have made possible the collection of feedback in dubious quantity. State-of-the-art technological systems and applications, monitored by artificial intelligence, ensure limitless benefit in terms of human connectivity solutions. But this connectivity comes at a price. Feedback can be repercussive. Our *community standards and practices* ensure individuals remain shielded from any and all feedback deemed to be traumatic by a committee of their peers."

"Draw back the curtain. Draw back the curtain that I may see," Zora repeated to herself, only now less intensely.

∽

"Now, if you don't mind," continued the presenter, "We are going to enact a series of roleplays in groups. These roleplaying activities are designed to provide a safe space in which to practice feedback delivery."

Then he stopped abruptly:

"There is supposed to be a volunteer here from the university this evening to help with the papers. I'm afraid—*or is she here by chance?* Miss Weaver, I believe it was? Miss Weaver? Are you here?"

"*I am.* I am Zora—*uhm*—Miss Weaver right here."

Zora stood up, straightening her O'Neill-brand Ambrosio Light Orange High-Low Maxi skirt nervously.

"Hello?" The presenter put his hand to his brow to avert the fluorescent glare.

"Yes, hello. I can help you pass out the papers. I am Miss Weaver."

Zora straightened herself. The fashion of the season had been black yoga pants, tube tops, and oversized jean jackets; and bare midriffs were also a big thing this autumn. But as this was a curricular event, Zora had decided to dress rather more tastefully. Her dress was a shade or two lighter than carnelian. It displayed perfectly where her blonde-tipped ringlets met the cinnamon skin of her shoulders, where the curves of Zora's guitar could be held in the ways that would lead to the production of the finest music.

A middle-aged woman in dreadlocks set with natural mordants approached Zora with a thick stack of packets. The woman wore a navy blue "*Volunteer*" t-shirt with a horribly designed insignia. The aberration of the t-shirt was somewhat soothed, thought Zora, by the woman's fashionably-pleated pink pants and a matching shade of lipstick. "One to each participant," said the woman as she handed the heavy stack to Zora.

As Zora distributed the packets to the somewhat sparse group of attendees, the dreadlocked woman followed, noticeably monitoring Zora's progress.

"Like this?" Zora asked facetiously, though still simpering enough so the woman couldn't be sure.

"Yes," answered the woman with the dreadlocks as she continued to follow.

The man in the front had continued his presentation:

"You will notice in the packet that the first roleplay activity is a fun one. The setting will enable us to practice facilitating a focused discussion."

After the packets had been distributed to all fifteen or so of the attendees, Zora and the woman again found themselves near the table in the back of the room.

"My name is Krystal Davis," offered the woman. "What we do now is wait until the end of Dr. Dinkelstein's seminar, then we collect the packets when they're done."

∾

The seminar went on a long time and there were somehow quite a number of entirely distinct, yet altogether quite similar roleplay activities. Zora closed and reopened her book in the back of the room, every so often running her eyes over a particular line of text without reading. Meanwhile the seminar dragged on:

"Your answers and assessments are essential to our enterprise. Upon collection, your completed packets and their contents will be technologically screened and analyzed, corrected but not over-corrected, then assigned easily recognizable and consistent adjectives to properly convey your character. Adjectives such as *excellent, wonderful,* and *stupendous,* will be agreed upon as key performance indicators according to our peer-reviewed ranking system. This system is monitored by a committee of experts to ensure that all approved feedback adjectives denote appropriate levels of support, and, conversely, that they allay any unnecessary feedback distress."

"This is when we collect the packets for Professor Dinkelstein," Krystal Davis nudged Zora.

Zora collected the packets from the participants and placed them next to the free coffee on the table at the back of the room. Once Dr. Dinkelstein and all the seminar participants had left, Krystal Davis allowed Zora her leave as well.

～

Krystal took the packets from the table and walked them into a small lobby behind the seminar hall, where rested an art nouveau sofa with distinctive, bun foot petals. Above the sofa were several large posters of a much younger Dr. Dinkelstein, smiling broad smiles, holding stacks of roleplay packets like the ones, according to recent changes in policy, that Krystal Davis was about to send unceremoniously through the shredder.

Five

*L*eaves fell. The seasons changed. Callous and self-serving is how the actions and attitudes of young people can sometimes be interpreted, and whether or not this system of social points is a product of the patriarchy, remains debatable. Zora Weaver, even as an involved member of Health and Wellness, remained detached. This is always an easier task for a minority within an entity; fundamental differences in nature ensure that a minority within a social whole can never become completely immersed. Zora recalled Lia Barnes, the only other black girl in her H&W rush class. Lia had mistakenly tried to compare, and even, at times, compete in the specialized system of womanhood for which MacKenzie Benoit and others were expressly trained. Lia Barnes, perhaps out of her own best interest, had not lasted long nor happily as a Health and Wellness house member.

For these reasons along with others, Zora spent her free time outdoors whenever the sometimes foggy and misty weather of the Central California coast would allow. She cherished her frequent afternoon visits to the university arboretum, where, in the Australia Garden, beneath the Banksias and the

Bog Gums, there was a wooden table where she liked to sit and write. The Fire-adapted Banksias were by far her favorites. She felt their serotinous essence to be the most aligned to her quest for a personal philosophy. The seeds of this particular tree require wildfire to germinate. They remain dormant in the earth for decades, waiting for a fire catastrophe to emerge.

Sometimes, early in the morning on weekends, before the garden gates were open, Zora hiked to the other side of campus, where the redwoods, in clusters and groves, shot toward the effervescence of the blue sky. This was another quiet place to be alone and to write, where Zora often reclined on a bed of soft needles in the sun-dappled ochre.

～

In joining Health and Wellness, Zora found an easy and pre-packaged means of connection. Superficial as the house was, she wasn't bothered. Zora was fit and enjoyed exercise to be certain, but in these activities, as in writing, Zora usually preferred to be alone. As much as she was indifferent to the structural and political churning involved in being an H&W girl, she did enjoy the yoga classes, her only regularly-scheduled H&W obligation aside from the monthly chapter meetings. The classes kept her fit and in tune with what was going on in the house to the extent that it might be necessary. The internship at the Soldiers' Center offered an opportunity for escape. Here she photocopied packets for Dr. Dinkelstein; once provided an impromptu audience of one for an especially verbose presenter named Qdora when no one else bothered to show up for their talk on Black Quantum Futurism; and learned to brew the coffee, all under the gimlet eye of her ever-present minder, Krystal Davis.

Not every event at the center was enjoyable. Specific presenters and participants called on Zora to exercise varying degrees of caution. There was the Spaniard from the university who gave monthly historical presentations. He had once slammed a heavy tome on the lectern in an effort to startle an absent-minded Zora back into absorption. Then there were the ancient seamen and paratroopers, with crumbs in their beards and crust forming at the sides of their mouths. Zora made sure to always keep a safe distance, and did her best to ignore their unabashed, sensual staring.

Aside from the many inconveniences, Zora appreciated her role at the Soldiers' Center. Philosophers have very little interest in the temporal, the changeable, the unfixed. In their professional and personal lives, they most often seek the absolute. Zora's internship afforded her an extra few hours a week of relative solitude and independence, away from the other students her age—away from Health and Wellness—her reading and writing interrupted only by the occasional, somewhat predictable requests for administration.

∾

Another member of the sophomore class of Health and Wellness was faring altogether much worse. Weiwei Li did not apply for the Wellness Officer position left vacant when Kayla Arroyo and Pilates lost out to Emma Swain and Mindful

Meditation. Over the course of the next several weeks, she stopped attending class.

At night Weiwei wandered downtown, past the used car lots and the beachy shops filled with holiday shoppers on vacation from places like Pittsburgh and St. Louis. Pleasant couples and families huddled around heat lamps slurping bowlfuls of chowder. There were panhandling homeless souls, too, watching the diners with jealousy and scorn. Weiwei passed the student bars and the pizza shops, two old cinema houses, a hotel with retro surfboards on display in the window. She walked down the cliff drive, under the palms and the cypress, alone, listening to the otherworldly churning of the surf.

At last, there was nowhere left for Weiwei to go but to the end of the wharf, where fish scales and muddy entrails seemed suitable company. There, she sat and gazed out into the distance at a single, flashing point of light as it was every-so-often obscured by the long breaks making their way in to shore.

∽

Like she knew she was supposed to do, Weiwei tried to find help. She was directed, via automated hotline, to the Office of the Assistant Dean for Student Life, Last Names A-M. A woman with a shrill voice answered on Weiwei's third call. The almost eerie tone of her voice reminded Weiwei of an aunt of hers who had been prescribed regular, heavy doses of anti-depressants.

"I would be delighted to schedule an appointment for you with Assistant Dean Tidris. Let me just consult her calendar.

We are always here to help. How about two weeks from this Tuesday?"

"Is there anything sooner?" Weiwei asked meekly.

"No, I'm afraid not. Dean Tidris is at the National Conference for Student Advisors this week. The week after that, she's *O-O-O* in Hawaii. May I trouble you for the precise nature of your request? We are always here to help."

"I've just been having some feelings—"

"Ah! Feelings," the woman interrupted. *"Yes, no problem at all.* That will be University Counseling Services you'll want."

Weiwei was given a phone number for another automated hotline, which led, in several more days, to her participation in a student support group.

~

The student support group was held in the evening in an inconspicuous classroom in the Cognitive Sciences Building. The sidelights were taped-over with copy paper; inside, eight chairs were set in a rough circle. One young man, a freshman with dark hair, was speaking:

"My roommate is sick so I'm worried I'm going to catch something from him. I haven't been really sick for a while, which is good, I guess, except for my lactose intolerance. I get so upset sometimes because no one really seems to care about my lactose intolerance. No matter how many times I tell people, even my closest friends and family, they're always still trying to get me to try cheese or milkshakes or whatever. Then, when I remind them of my *allergy*, they say something like, 'It's ok, you can just *tell me* if you don't want to try something.' But I *do* want to try. I just *can't*. That's what I've been telling them all along except nobody's listening. *Why can't anyone understand? Why does nobody care?* I used to be able to drink milk and eat cheese, but then, when I got a little older, I started getting all bloated and crampy every time I tried it. Last year, back at my high school, the Orchestra all chipped in and bought me a huge sheet cake for my birthday. *Butter cream icing!* Can you believe that? I couldn't even eat it. Goddamnit I had to sit there and watch everyone else eat *my* birthday cake and I couldn't even have any. Someone eventually felt bad for me and gave me a box of old, crummy raisins and that's about all I got for my birthday.

"Plus, my friend Raimundo's father passed away. Really horrible. I'd never met him before, but Raimundo talked about him every once in a while. Really bad colon cancer. Raimundo found out and then his dad up and died within three weeks. I only knew all of this because Raimundo called me and we talked about it.

"Oh, and I have a work-study at the library on weekends. I reshelve books and sometimes work at the media counter. So anyway, no one will talk to me there, *ever*. I'm the kind of person who needs people to talk to me, you know. And every week I go in, and none of my coworkers will talk to me. I try to start conversations and they just slough me off. It's horrible. Last week, I even brought in a dozen donuts for everyone to share, thinking that might start some conversation. I said, 'Hey everyone, I brought in some free donuts. They're over here on the media counter if you want to stop by for one during your shift tonight.' *Nobody came.* Nobody came the whole night. Not even for a donut. I just threw them all away."

"There," said the facilitator once the young man with the dark hair in the black t-shirt had finished. "Now I'm sure that everyone feels much better."

But Weiwei Li wasn't sure what she felt as she stepped out of the Department of Cognitive Sciences and into the darkness of night.

Six

single, small craft shone a light as it sailed into the harbor. The last pink on the horizon rusted copper, then crimson, before seeping away into the maritime dusk. Like the sombre bark of the sea lions as it carried through downtown and up the hill, the young women of Health and Wellness found their way to the yoga studio.

The studio boasted a broad, hardwood floor made from the longest and most expensive planks available. There was a long barre, imported from Paris, and, in a far corner, a stack of pillows and cushions for whenever chapter meetings were in order and people had to sit. The studio had been a gift from a house member's father who had owned a bank. It was the most impressive room in an otherwise impressive house, one in good repair—built on a corner property. It lit up even the street from the track lighting of the studio and all the energy of the fit girls working out inside.

The air in the studio on this evening was thick with the aroma of lavender and magnolia, citron and cardamom. It was the Tuesday following the first long weekend of the semester, and the girls of Health and Wellness—most of them anyway—were convened for Emma Swain's Mindful Meditation in its coveted five-thirty time slot.

However there was very little mindfulness and absolutely no meditation as a result of the news. Information from university administration was scant, but had been independently confirmed and verified by at least three sources. Weiwei Li was dead, found by her parents at home in Southern California, sometime over the long weekend.

~

"What did her parents say?"

"I don't know, I just heard the news."

"I heard she was thinking about going out for the Wellness Officer position."

"I heard that too. But then she decided to focus more on her studies instead."

"It's just awful. *Horrible*. I feel so bad for her family."

"Did anyone hear why she did it?"

"Maybe something that happened at the water polo house?"

To those in the know, these last words were designed to end all conversation on the matter, not to be uttered aloud unless it was certain that all in one's company *could* understand and *would* understand the many implicated shades of meaning. Each member of Health and Wellness had, or were sure to have their crisis at the water polo house. And if it wasn't water polo, it'd surely be basketball or football or lacrosse.

"Where is MacKenzie Benoit? Someone asked. "I thought she was definitely going to be here tonight?"

~

At precisely that moment, MacKenzie arrived, dressed for the occasion in *Lulu Lemon*, all black. MacKenzie's mahogany hair was expressly coiffed. A lapel pin affixed to her yoga attire signified a broken heart circumscribed by gold-leaf edges. She gauged the air of the studio, the relative proportions of cardamom and sage underneath the hot lights.

"I'm sure you've all heard?"

All those present were still too paralyzed by the sudden news to speak.

"It's really too bad what happened at the water polo house. I heard Weiwei was there the Thursday before the long weekend—at their party. I know she'd recently recommitted to her studies—poor Weiwei—so I'm sure she was just trying to let off some steam."

"Weiwei was such a good student, and such a model for what we Health and Wellness girls ought to be," someone piped up from a remote corner of the room.

"Yes, Weiwei was completely committed to Health and Wellness. I know as a fact that she even considered going out for the open Wellness Officer position before she decided to recommit to her studies. Weiwei Li really had it together—a class act all the way—she had her priorities straight right up until the end. Poor Weiwei—"

"I heard maybe she was having trouble making fitness a priority," someone offered.

"Oh, but haven't we all had trouble prioritizing from time to time? I can't say exactly why she chose to focus on her studies and not to go out for Wellness Officer. I always assumed that was something between Weiwei and her academic advisor. In the final analysis—*oh*, that sounds so trite to say now! But— in the final analysis—I suppose it's a good thing for Health and Wellness that poor Weiwei didn't go out after all. She was so popular and well-liked; she would have surely won. Then what a mess we'd be in now.

"Fortunately or unfortunately, I have experience like this from my junior year at Academy Hall. One of the girls in my class committed suicide. *There*, it took me a long time to be able to say it so matter of factly. And—*well then*—as a class, we had to be very careful not to let the unfortunate actions of one individual reflect less than favorably on us all. It's the same for us here now, I'm afraid. We of course need to be there for Weiwei's family during their trying time, and the Board is reaching out to university administration to provide our full support as a house. But some of the other houses may try to use this as an opportunity to steal away some of our top pledges this year and maybe even next. We can't let them do that. Not to mention what this could do to our reputation in general around campus. We'll have to be more unified than ever as we remember our sister, Weiwei, and put forth a positive face on the future of our house for our organization and in her memory.

"Fortunately for us, we're in good hands with the Board, and we'll all be the healthiest versions of our best possible selves thanks in part to our newly-elected Wellness Officer, Zora Weaver. Zora, are you here, darling?" MacKenzie didn't feign to wait for a response before continuing: "Zora has her work cut out for her in keeping us all at peak fitness during this trying time.

"In addition, I've also asked Zora to help me plan a small remembrance ceremony in honor of Weiwei. *House members only.* I know Zora was just as shaken up by all of this horrible news as me, so I think it will be cathartic for us to work together on our remembrance of our friend and suitemate."

~

Outside the studio, the haloed moon lit the hillside. Planets and stars peeked out from behind the illuminated clouds. A cool breeze blew in from the north, bringing with it the first stings of winter.

Seven

The Institute was a world-renowned spiritual center on the bluffs by the sea, so naturally Zora had been drawn to it. For years growing up in Berkeley she had circled it closely, drawn to the idea of the place, wondering the best way to make a proper entrance.

Zora had never been able to bring herself to drop in on the *"private sessions"* as described by a cryptic sign on the property's gate, and there was little she could tell from the Institute's altogether vague web presence. She had never even brought herself to call the front desk. Yet it was not without knowledge of a vague connection between the two places, that our hero had chosen her internship at the Soldiers' Memorial Services Center.

The connection was murky, to be certain. No one really knew its essence for sure, and anyone who did, never spoke about it directly—not to her, anyway. So Zora accepted her difficult, meandering path to the knowledge never quite at hand. She based her willingness on a stubborn assertion that a difficult path to tread may be the one best worth treading. Zora felt the Institute would be a place to aspire to even greater thoughts, above the blur of the university and the city and the chaos below.

∾

Since the beginning of her internship, and in truth, since the beginning of the internship application process the previous spring, Zora's attraction to the Institute and everything for which it stood had intensified. Her desire became thirsty and vulgar. She sought out scraps of relevant information at the bookstore, at libraries on campus, and from a careful examination of photos culled from the society pages. She arranged for private meetings with professors she thought might be in the know.

∾

"*Umm*, I don't know about that anymore," was the response when Zora had taken a chance to ask Krystal Davis.

But days later, after an especially long and boring session at the Soldiers' Center, Krystal slipped Zora a card. It read, in bold, black lettering:

The Institute

Staff

Tuesday, November 17, 2020

5-9 pm

Building 8

"You can count this toward your regular hours if you'd like to work. Same deal. Help to distribute the packets and maybe serve some hors d'oeuvres after that if they need extra help."

This was exactly what Zora had been waiting for. This means to enter the mysterious Institute seemed more than fitting. Perhaps the oddness (of it all) was to be expected. She made her arrangements to arrive by the Route 1 bus on the appointed date at the appointed time.

～

Many a philosopher knows the value of perspective, and Zora had it in mind to use this journey to the Institute both as credit for her internship, and as her own, personal inspiration for the few lines of remembrance she was expected to provide for Weiwei's ceremony. Thinkers can be selfish in this way to be certain, and as she traveled north on the bus, Zora clutched her notebook and two bound volumes for reference, daydreaming about any inspiration she might find.

～

There, several miles north of the city, north of the strawberry fields and of Panther Beach, was the gated drive that led to the hallowed place. The main complex of The Institute rested on a low-lying hill beyond a collection of interspersed lagoons, only meters beyond a stunning white-sand, and much-revered, national beach.

A pastiche of swooping, winged buildings in beach tones ranging from cedar to blue-grey dotted the hillside. It was low tide and long-legged shorebirds stalked the bottoms of the mudflat lagoons.

Zora stepped in from the beach at the bus stop. She followed a sandy path until she was met by a series of wooden totems. These extended in a semicircle, one after another, each one higher than the previous. Across the tallest three beams was fastened a carved sign. It read:

The Institute

Est. 1959

A bridge constructed from upcycled wharf wood led across the most immediate of the lagoons. Sea gulls sat on the railings. Terns screeched in the sky. Great tubes of agave with their phallic protuberances formed a tunnel to a diverse botanical garden, and, beyond that, at the top of the hill, a bronze gong hung from a natural, knotted segment of tree branch.

Zora expected the intellectual atmosphere here to be wholly the opposite from that at the university. Whereas the architecture and public spaces at the university seemed to be the grand, crucial ingredient to all the academic happenings therein, these strange and resilient styles near the sea seemed extensions of the natural landscape as carved by loving admirers.

A sign read:

Here by the sea it is easy

to listen to the waves and feel their pulse.

The ocean is our connection to a greater consciousness.

We feel it here and _____

A curious-looking man with dreadlocks fashioned in both his hair and his beard was seated in front of this sign with legs-crossed, whittling away at the blank.

"What are you carving?" Zora stopped to ask.

"Oh, we're not quite certain yet," replied the strangely-bearded man. "I'm really just practicing my technique." His eyes glimmered in the last of the day's fading light. "Either '*We feel it here and interpret its meaning*,' or '*We feel it here and harness its power*.' Or something different altogether if one or another of the committees decides."

∽

It was dusk now and the sound of the breakers churning pierced the evening, far down the hillsides of pine and palm and eucalyptus.

Eight

uilding Eight was the first building at the top of the trail, and the one immediately next to the gong Zora had spied from below. Zora knew this was the place when she got there, because there was a door open and a light shining inside, which made it appear like the right place to go. Beneath the low-hanging vines of passion fruit and granadilla, Zora was showered by a soft music emanating from a somewhere she couldn't quite decipher. Here a guest services attendant sat behind a tall, white counter appointed in the most modern of tastes. A second attendant was answering a call:

"Thank you, Doctor Foxglove. Yes, the scenery really is quite astounding, isn't it? I'm so glad you're enjoying it. Yes, we are all very proud of it. *Oh*, what's that, Doctor Foxglove? Oh no, I'm afraid there aren't any tee times available for same day appointments. *No*, not even for you. Perhaps I could put you in touch with our pro shop, who will be able to schedule you at the perfect time. Yes, I'm sure you'll see the time that they choose will be the perfect one indeed, well in accordance with your schedule, the weather and the luxurious surroundings. Just let the pro shop know your availability and they'll be happy to arrange it all. Yes, I'm sure it will be to your satisfaction, Doctor Foxglove. Thank you and have a healthy day."

"Welcome to the Institute," the young woman behind the tall desk peered down at Zora. "May I help you?"

Zora flashed the card provided by Krystal Davis. The young woman behind the desk nodded to a door marked *Intake*, and indicated for Zora to enter. The soft music continued here, and Zora found herself in a waiting room, one surrounded on all sides by glass-walled cubicles, each with a service desk visible inside.

A robotic sensor eased down from one of the glass walls. It scanned Zora's body and administered a health check. The check cleared momentarily, and Zora was instructed to enter Bay Six.

∾

After passing a vacuum-sealed doorway into one of the cubicles, Zora was at once met by a guest services attendant wearing a white satin uniform designed expressly for the position. The only manner in which his uniform was different from any of the others in any way, was that his trim was green, while other options may have been red or blue.

"Would you like a printout of your biometric screening along with our recommendations for your ideal diet and activities?"

Before Zora had a chance to answer, the gentleman pressed a blue button on the desk and a single, glossy sheet was berthed from a slot facing Zora. "Now, how may I be of assistance?" He asked, looking so directly at Zora it was uncomfortable for her to bear.

"I was given this card," Zora answered as she reached into her pocket.

The man interrupted: "A card, *a card!* In that case, Ms. Weaver, these biometric statistics will certainly be of great use to you both today during your visit and long after." He looked at Zora quizzically. "So what are you here to do, exactly?"

Now Zora was the quizzical one. She responded: "To work? I was given this card—"

"Everyone who comes to the Institute is here to *work*, Ms. Weaver. The question is, *on what* were you hoping to work? There must have been something or other or it's unlikely you would have been invited. The Sage only very infrequently suffers from lapses in judgement."

Zora thought for a moment. This was an altogether strange development.

"Well, I guess I was planning to write a few words of remembrance for my friend—"

"*Remembrances, writing-of—*" The man pressed a touchscreen and was directed through a series of prompts that looked to Zora like the silly compliance quizzes required by the university.

"First, I must save and document all of your essential data," said the attendant before spending a somewhat inordinate amount of time punching at the screen. Finally, he asked: "Your friend's name?"

"My—*what*?" Zora was wholly confused by the nature of the question. *Why was he asking this?* This all seemed so oddly out of place compared with what Zora might otherwise have been expecting.

"Weiwei Li," she decided to respond, but only once she had regained her composure.

"For—*ahh*—Weiwei's words of remembrance, what sorts of words did you have in mind? Flowery, of course, but perhaps not too much. Of course so much depends on the audience, your relationship with the deceased and your personal taste. Some invitees find the process too time-consuming or otherwise onerous, but those who accept all the teachings as directed by the Sage are the ones who achieve the longest-lasting results.

"The Institute was established to allow for the refinement and overall betterment of our members and their guests. We believe our processes allow for a maximum benefit, and that this benefit flows from within oneself out, and throughout all of one's life's works. The determination of one's path is all quite individualized, as you'll see. But I'm cautious to say that even though every trainee's plan comes from within the themself alone, the vessel for each plan is the Institute, and the teachings of the Sage are the great emulsifier.

"Your invitation does not include a personal one-on-one with the Sage, I'm afraid," he added. "Most who are fortunate enough to receive an audience with *Her Eminence* find it to be quite enlightening.

"At the Institute our aim is to lead you toward a more perfect version of yourself. Once you become your personal best, even the most minuscule task in your personal or professional life will miraculously fall into place.

"Of course, the magic was really within you all along; we're just here to help you piece it all together. What you've received from Krystal is the *Perfect Version* gift card, good for two evening sessions here at the Institute to help you accomplish your goal and *or* goals. Tell me, were you very close with—*ahh*—Weiwei, *yes*, Weiwei? Were you two very close?"

"No, I'm afraid not. That's probably why I've been having so much trouble writing her remembrance."

"What was Weiwei's line of work? If you don't mind me asking—"

"She was a student—a Liberal Education major."

"Yes, in that case I'm sure we'll be able to help. Please, if you will—"

The attendant stood and showed Zora around to his side of the desk, behind which there was a glass door which slid open automatically at his gesture.

"Here at the Institute, we specialize in honing you to be the most perfect you that you could ever possibly be—"

~

Zora followed the man in the uniform into a darkened space that looked nothing at all like what she'd seen from the other side of the glass. The ambiance was one of soothing Asian flute music and electric candlelight. Finely manicured turf soothed any aching toes or joints; stalking birds of paradise peeked around every corner in the dim light. The air tasted of pure oxygen, and Zora found the humidity to be set at the most suitable level for deep breathing.

"Your particular package starts with a complimentary tour of our facilities," said the guest services attendant. "Let me ask you: *How do you typically like to do your thinking?*"

"Alone. Outdoors, but still comfortable," answered Zora without hesitation.

"*Ah, well, yes then,* this will certainly be the perfect place for you to write your words—"

"I want to see it all."

"Yes, I've arranged for one of our guides to provide you with a complete tour of the amenities and privileges just as soon as we've finished *intake.* To your right here and below, you will see the squash courts, followed by the cardiovascular gym, the strength training gym, our Olympic-sized indoor-outdoor pool with diving platforms and jacuzzi, then our exquisite lobby, with its famous picture window looking out over majestic Hole Thirteen of *The Bluffs,* our award-winning, world-class golf course, not to be confused with *Bayside Lagoons,* our other world-class, award-winning course. Was your friend Weiwei any special religion? Did she have overt sexual preferences that could easily be described by one of the twelve types outlined here?" The guest services attendant in green trim handed Zora a card with busy printing, but the lighting was too dim to read it.

"Buddhist—I think. Cisgender woman."

"There are prayer spaces and reliquaries here enough to accommodate every religious persuasion: meditation rooms, yoga studios, a full spa—our hiking and running trails have been 3-D modeled by every major fitness equipment manufacturer for use in their interactive displays; not to mention the beach and our private scuba lagoon."

"But—I don't understand—I'm only preparing to speak for a small collection of friends at our university's Health and Wellness house."

"Perhaps a secular ceremony would be best, in that case."

"I think Weiwei and the others might appreciate a few words about the importance of fitness."

"Then I believe we really are in exactly the perfect place for your goals, Ms. Weaver. Tell me, was Weiwei very mindful of her body?"

"She was a member of the Health and Wellness house, yes."

"That's wonderful—*I'm sure*—but are you certain she was completely focused on her health and well-being?"

"I can assure you she was quite fit in some ways."

An image flashed suddenly and involuntarily across Zora's mindscape, an image of Weiwei Li at the center of the sectional sofa in their apartment suite. Weiwei was there, over-weight with rolls of flab hanging out from the undersides of her favorite sweatshirt. She was drunk but demanding more alco-hol, scooping out the innards of a gallon tub of cookie dough ice cream with an oversized spoon.

"And, Ms. Weaver, forgetting for a moment about your dearly-departed friend Weiwei, what would you say you most need to work on as an individual in order to accomplish your goals?"

Zora thought for a moment. She wasn't sure if the guest services attendant meant this in terms of writing Weiwei's words of remembrance, or just in general with respect to her own life. She decided it didn't matter before answering abruptly:

"Restraint."

Nine

" As you can see from this wing of the Institute, our whole complex is connected through the beautifully trellised breezeways, and, although you can't see them now, also underground through a system of natural sandstone caves. The caves double to house our collection of libraries: the humanities library, the medical library, the technology library, the medical technology library—*you get the idea.* Our impressive collection of antiquities is in the East Wing, and an infused purewater bar is here at this corner in case you ever get thirsty. We take hydration very seriously here, Ms. Weaver.

"I know this next bit may seem counter-intuitive, but it's absolutely imperative. Let's try to forget about your friend for a moment as we undertake this process. I can assure you this is the only way to attain the peak performance required to perform this, or any other endeavor at your absolute best."

The guest services attendant and Zora made several turns and presently came to the end of a hallway, beyond which were clearly visible the sauna facilities and the entrance to the changing rooms. There they stood before a large dais replete with a touchscreen displaying the overarching categories of luxury Institute services.

"Please feel free to peruse our catalog while I locate an appropriately gendered guide to continue our tour. Please also feel free also to select your first several activities if you find anything that inspires your fancy."

~

The attendant left the room and Zora took her time in browsing. She enjoyed having a break from what she presumed to be nothing more than a grandiose sales pitch. She swiped through the categories. They reminded her of registering for classes, or of choosing Health and Wellness fitness activities on the first day of the semester. It would be important, she felt, to partake of activities she would not normally have a chance to do otherwise. Why order pasta with red sauce at a restaurant, she thought, when she could just as easily make that at home?

After what ended up being a somewhat agonizing decision, Zora decided on a tour of the Near-Asian collection and a deep tissue massage, followed by a virtual golf lesson in one of the sensory bays.

"Are you sure this is going to help me write Weiwei's remembrance? I actually haven't scheduled any time for that at all."

"Last week there was an invitee who wanted to work up the courage to leave her longtime, live-in boyfriend. After a massage, a nutrition consultation, a cooking lesson and a private audience with the Sage, she actually decided to marry the guy." Here the attendant momentarily slipped from his polished routine. "Sometimes you just have to go with it. Take my advice and leave it in the hands of our knowledgeable staff. The Sage knows the path and was put here on this planet in order to help you and many others like you find it."

"Well, that's nice to think about, I guess."

"Oh, I completely agree. Isn't it though? Tell, me, will you have the need for any tailoring while you are here? Our tailoring facility specializes in the bespoke. Here at the Institute, we realize that your event may require the perfect set of fineries for you to present at your very best. This being the case, rest assured, our fabrics are the absolute finest—imported from Italy, Dubai, Spain, India, and Thailand—something for every taste and style indeed. For your skin tone, I would say bright colors would be best, Thailand or India maybe, the brighter the better; pastels—yellow, blue, orange. *Yes*, that would really *pop*. Depending on what you decide as far as tailoring, our cosmeticians can handle the rest. Personal styling is also included, of course. We've already obtained all of your measurements and can make fashion suggestions based on the data."

Zora took the man's advice and just went with it:

"I suppose it might be fitting for me to look my very best out of respect for Weiwei and the others in attendance. Perhaps some bespoke yoga wear and something slightly fancier to wear to any after parties? Are you quite certain you have my accurate measurements?"

"*Oh, quite.* However, if there are any particulars accordinging to your tastes or desires, we could leave a special note for the tailors."

Here the attendant was interrupted as he made use of an earbud. "I'm afraid the tour has been delayed," he apologized to Zora before leading her through a doorway and into a stall well. The Asian spa music now gave way to a sort of cosmic electronica, the same sort as played by the campus radio station very early on Sunday mornings. They walked up one flight and the guest services attendant opened a fire door at the second-floor landing. There he asked a surprised colleague, "Is there an unoccupied cultivation room or vestibule at present?"

"Only Sea Jasmine."

"*Sea Jasmine, yes.* Thank you. Please, after me, Ms. Weaver."

~

The two walked past a long row of doors with translucent but not transparent windows, like so many rooms in a karaoke parlor. When they reached the door next to which a small, faux-gold placard read *Sea Jasmine*, the attendant stepped aside and allowed Zora to enter.

Here she discovered a small chamber, not altogether unlike an examination room at the doctor's office, or what Zora imagined a cabin on a cruise ship must be like. There was a chaise lounge; a cushioned, all-purpose chair; and a desk, one similar to the desks found in all the intake cubicles. The familiar touchscreens displayed the Institute's catalog of services on the desk and at a console on the wall.

"Ms. Weaver, it now appears that one of our guides is available to meet with you to further distinguish your preferences. Before I take your leave to attend to other invitees, is there anything else at all for which I may be of assistance?"

Zora thought for a moment, but she was now only certain that she wasn't at all certain what to think. She still expected this whole operation to be a pitch to sell her more sessions. She imagined it must now necessarily go something like:

> *Have you considered making the multifold benefits of the Institute a permanent or semi-permanent part of your betterment lifestyle, Ms. Weaver? I know it all must seem a trifle odd that in order to solve the minor inconveniences of life, all you ever needed to do was focus absolutely all of your efforts on self-betterment, but we have found this much to be true—*
>
> *Once you progress through your own personalized program, everything will feel and appear quite differently. The benefits of being invited young and starting early are immense, both in terms of the self-betterment, but also in terms of the spiritual, and—more often than not—the financial benefits an Institute membership can bring. You are still a young woman, Ms. Weaver, with a whole career ahead of you. Just consider the networking connections alone*

you stand to gain from membership. Think of it in terms of any other well-being policy or account; like retirement benefits, health insurance or auto care. Believe it! Becoming your best possible self is actually more important— not merely on par with, all these other import- ant necessities of life.

Somewhat disappointingly to Zora, the attendant's parting words were rather more droll:

"Individual cultivation consultations are provided in cultivation rooms such as this one. The cultivation consultant will join you shortly. Please feel free to refamiliarize yourself with our vast catalog of services and the room controls while you wait."

～

The guest services attendant made his exit and Zora tried instantly to forget any specifics about him. She was convinced these types were holographic representations of people as created by investment firms and Silicon Valley, and nothing or very little more. For someone more hinged to a time and a place, it may have proven useful to differentiate between such individuals; but to the eye of a reticent, young philosopher, the guest services attendant had been just one limb of some ever-regenerating Eastern deity. Zora could be served breakfast in the East Bay, led to the examination room in Palo Alto, then be sold a ticket at the box office in Saratoga; all by the same uniformed, convenient person. If Zora took the time to get to know any one of these renderings, she would encounter the same, contrived talking points and leading questions—like the hook of a popular but new song to which one finds themselves singing before they've even bothered to learn the title.

Wearing a uniform would be the *easy way*. Zora sought the unknown and the unknowable. She did not fear the far reaches of the corridor with no end. She sought out every next adventure with the same spirit which had led her to the Institute in the first place.

And it was her adventurous soul that filled Zora with anxious, empty dread the moment Krystal Davis entered the room, providing a heavy dose of reality to a scene that henceforth had left Zora's mind swimming in a sea of intoxicant liquids.

Ten

The tips of Krystal's dreads were dipped in red and she wore an exquisitely tailored black pantsuit with long, thin lapels. She appeared to Zora as if wholly resurfaced with moisturizing lotions and mascara and beautifying treatments. Her lips, owing to the work of the master cosmeticians, were painted in the exactly-fashionable shade of red to match both the tips of her provocative hair and the cat's eye makeup sweeping out magnificently toward her temples.

Krystal's nose was finely-figured. Her cheeks sat high and round. Her eyes were hewn of reflective onyx. Whether or not it was the lighting, Zora couldn't be sure, but Krystal's skin seemed to glow in tones of warm rosewood. Zora caught herself as she stopped breathing with surprise.

∾

"How did Weiwei pass?" Krystal asked, already acutely aware of more about Zora than had been discussed during their brusque personal interactions at the Soldiers' Center.

"Suicide, I think."

"You think?"

"University administration wasn't exactly forthcoming about the details."

"I suppose that's not unusual. The Sage, in her infinite wisdom, tells us *we are all but leaves on the same branch, branches on the same tree.* It's disheartening to hear about the loss of a friend at such a young age."

"What is it you do here at the Institute?" Zora asked.

"I volunteer here just as I volunteer at the Soldiers' Memorial Services Center. My wife is a veteran, and, as a result, she receives excellent medical care and access to free services just like the seminar program we manage together there. Volunteering is the least I can do to give back. *Tell me,* were you very close with Weiwei?"

Zora's reaction betrayed more than she would have desired, and that reaction alone was enough to prompt Krystal's next inquiry:

"*If not,* I'm wondering why you've been elected to write her remembrance ceremony?"

"I was nominated by someone—It's largely a social duty."

"Was Weiwei a good, close friend would you say?"

"She wasn't a *bad* friend, but I guess I don't really know that much about her—"

"Distinguishing between leaves on the same tree is often difficult, especially for other leaves."

"I'm not certain that either she or—I *are...were... is...*a leaf."

"We welcome skepticism here at the Institute. Skepticism is healthy, Ms. Weaver. If it weren't for a certain degree of skepticism indicated *by you to me* at the center, I find it unlikely you would have ever been identified and invited. The Sage specializes in skeptics. My wife was one of the first female soldiers trained by the armed forces to do the kind of work she did. Nearly stars and bars, and would have been too if she were a man, but in those days things were much different than they are now.

"I say this to say, my wife was more skeptical than most at the onset. Skepticism was an important part of her life's work. But *even she* was convinced after only a few sessions. Skeptics are our favorite invitees, Ms. Weaver; they give us the opportunity to showcase everything the Institute has to offer. If you would like, I'm sure I could find a time for you to hear my wife's testimonial. She keeps very busy and serves on a grand jury and several soldiers' affairs committees, including one at the Services Center. She is disabled and has been for some time. She has increasing difficulty getting around these days, but I'm sure we could still find a time for you two to meet if you are interested."

"No—*no thank you.* I don't think that will be necessary, not at this point anyway."

"No, of course not. First take a look around. Get to know the amenities. I can fill you in on all the pertinent details later."

"Well that is very reassuring."

"In time you'll come to see there's no limit to what you can absorb here, Zora. You'll see."

"I'm quite certain I've had enough to absorb today already."

"Certainly nothing like absorbing the recent loss of a personal acquaintance though, I'm sure. Many invitees seeking wisdom from the Sage are drawn at first by some horrible life event that's somehow affected—*usually negatively*, I hate to say it—their temporary state of being. Sometimes, there's nothing even the Sage can do. It's one of our maxims here at the Institute: *one must first be prepared to learn in order to be taught the way.* See and believe. The teachings of the Sage work miracles for anyone who's prepared to listen and try."

"I must note how great your respect for this—*Sage*—seems to be."

"She is a great philosopher," Ms. Weaver. "Perhaps the greatest living one—though I must admit frankly that she's the only one I've ever really met."

"*This does seem like an interesting place to do volunteer work.*"

"It is both an honor and a pleasure, I can assure you."

"May I ask how long you have been affiliated with the Institute?"

"Oh, it's been some time. More than just years—nearly a decade I should think.

"We are now nearing the end of our consultation," Krystal said. "Tell me, is there something in particular you'd like to convey about yourself by delivering Weiwei's words of remembrance? After all, you will still be here for a long time, and Weiwei is already gone. Often it takes difficult and painful realizations about the nature of our place in the universe for a person to become their best, personal selves and thereby accomplish all of their own, personal goals. I know this point of view can sound selfish at first, but once the realization occurs, it's a spiritual awakening, let me assure you. It's pure enrapturement, and maybe ascension to divinity to a certain degree—all at once for you—and all brought about by the way of the Sage."

"You'll have to forgive me if I'm not yet moved to the point of abstraction."

"Oh, and there's one additional point we seem to have neglected to ask—was that a deep tissue massage or a Swedish massage you preferred? We also have specialists in East Asian pressure points and acupuncture at the ready if you are so inclined."

"I'm not really sure of the difference."

"Let's do a one-hour Swedish massage. That will give you an introduction to the benefits of each type. We can save the acupuncture for another time. Jorge is on staff today and he is really quite the best. I'll arrange for him to be in this very room for you after your tour of the antiquities."

"How will I even know how to find my way back—or around this immense place at all?"

"Not to worry. We've arranged for guides every step of the way."

"When will I see you next?"

"Tuesday next week. Come just before sundown for your follow-up appointment; I'm not sure yet of the exact time. And feel free to select three more activities you might like to try. Can I offer a scheduled ride from campus when you come?"

"No—no thank you. I'll be fine taking the bus."

"Good," smiled Krystal, before leaving the room.

The familiar guest services attendant then returned. He said:

"Ms. Weaver, as it turns out, I will be providing your tour of our near-Asian collection. Many of the objects are really quite rare. We have wonderful calligraphic scrolls from the fourteenth century, pottery, amphora of various shapes and sizes, human remains…mummies, petroglyphs."

"Yes, that does sound like quite a lot to see. After all that, I'll surely be ready for a massage."

Eleven

here is not very much at all one can keep from a
roommate during sophomore year at university, and
soon enough Zora found herself obliged to explain everything to MacKenzie. MacKenzie had noted the slightly askew
hours of Zora's new internship. She had watched as Zora gazed
furtively out the window—this even more frequently than
usual. MacKenzie needed Zora to focus on Weiwei's ceremony
and other urgent Health and Wellness matters of concern.
Chloe McDougall had diarrhea and needed someone to teach
her regular Kundalini class, a large shipment of Pinot Gris had
mistakenly arrived in place of the rosé ordered by the social
committee. All those in the sistership would be expected to
perform a supportive role during this turbulent time.

"You should see the place," Zora gushed in a rare,
unguarded moment of pure excitement. "There were surfing
lessons and access to some of the best breaks on the north
coast, stand up paddle boarding—I played golf but I'm not
very good at that. Oh, and the food is wonderful. I only had
a chance to try some of the hors d'oeuvres, but I'm going to
ask to see the restaurant next time. The Institute's focus is on

total, personal wellness of both body and mind. I'm also keeping attuned to any ideas we might be able to introduce back at Health and Wellness."

MacKenzie seemed unimpressed:

"I just want *somebody* to teach Chloe's class, and *someone* to make sure Cassidy Granger doesn't drink all the Pinot before we get it sent back to the distributor. I don't know why Chloe eats from the vegan bar at the main refectory. I've told her a thousand times, you're better off going through the line and asking for sides of fruit and pasta. *You were invited somewhere fantastic.* That's wonderful for you, Zora. But we have *serious* issues here. Not all of us can be off surfing and trail running and sipping cocktails on oceanside balconies."

"MacKenzie, are you jealous?"

"Of course, I'm jealous. You were invited to a mysterious compound and pampered and fed hors d'oeuvres. There are attendants to give you massages and infused water. I *love* infused water. L-O-V-E, love! Go if you have to. You *were* invited. I didn't expect you would want to teach Kundalini for Chloe anyway."

~

That week, the girls of Health and Wellness offered their condolences to Weiwei's family, who arrived on campus to meet with the administration, and to collect Weiwei's things. MacKenzie Benoit took control of public relations, and with help from the other H&W girls so inclined, began preparations for the remembrance ceremony. Any of the Bigs who held a formal position in the house or the Littles who aspired to one, wanted a role in the proceedings.

"Someone needs to say a few words of remembrance," MacKenzie reminded Zora. "I'm not sure I'll be in any state to do it myself. I know you've been working on a few words. Please feel free to include any *joyful* sections from those philosophical books I see you toting around. I hope you're able to find the amazing sister we all knew—a strong, resilient, fit, and dedicated student, right up until the end."

"I'm not sure how strong she could have been—" Zora caught herself before quite saying.

"Yes, strong in character was our Weiwei. So strong that when her character came up against real problems, her character won out. *That was the problem.* Poor Weiwei. *Strong* Weiwei. What a fighter."

"Funny, I don't remember her ever signing up for kick-boxing class—"

"You need to produce *something*, Zora. We're counting on you. Maybe just find something Buddhist. What did her parents say? Weren't they going to something at a temple? Use something like that. If you don't want to speak at the ceremony, just write it and give it to me and I can read it for you. We need something to fill the five minutes between Hannah Morgan's cleansing ceremony and the suicide prevention workshop; it's more important than ever for you to show your sisterhood. It's not very much to do at all, considering the circumstances. The others and I are doing all the booking."

The *others* were not so involved as was MacKenzie, in her public relations role: choosing the invitees, sending out the invitations, setting the schedule. While Weiwei's remembrance ceremony at the house would be relegated to Health and Wellness members only, which Health and Wellness members exactly, remained at MacKenzie's sole discretion. Some of the Littles who were behind in their dues, or had neglected to attend the appropriate number of fitness classes, or had otherwise offended political sensibilities, were left off the final list.

After a long debate it was decided that Kayla Arroyo would be invited even in spite of the Caden Dunwoody affair, and that the offended party would be granted full use of the yoga studio for three hours on a Sunday night in January. This was so her boyfriend on the baseball team could hold a Super Bowl party, to which Kayla would not be invited.

∿

In chorus with these frenzied activities, Zora searched the apartment suite for something to spark an idea. Despite Weiwei's recommitment to her education, Zora couldn't exactly remember ever seeing Weiwei with a book. She was a listener—a very good listener—and a talker, but not so much a reader or a writer. Most of Weiwei's cherished belongings had already been collected by her grieving family members. What was left in her room were random pieces of computer miscellany and some clothes Zora remembered her wearing.

Zora tried to remember the first time she ever met Weiwei. It was at the end of freshman year in MacKenzie's room in Slater Quad. All the Slater girls were pregaming before going out for a night of drinking on Ocean Street. That night was a frenetic rush of bars and blurry nighttime lights. Within an hour, everyone had been separated. Zora ended up in the basement of the football house for a loud and altogether forgettable end to the evening. She didn't see Weiwei again until Spring Weekend, and then again once briefly at Campus Dance after that, but these end-of-the-year, madcap events were no place for serious discussion or truly getting to know one's peers.

~

In the end, Zora took her cue from a Religious Studies 058 course reader that had been left behind, forgotten in a nook Weiwei's desk. The lone, Eastern philosophy inclusion in the compilation had been highlighted, and it included some very pertinent verses about yoga. It wasn't Buddhist in a strict sense, but MacKenzie and the others wouldn't be likely to know or care. These were just a few of the highlighted words that had passed through Weiwei's world. Zora built up the content with a handful of related Vedic verses. She copied and pasted, then passed her completed assignment on to MacKenzie.

Twelve

Colonel Mickey "Mike," "Radar" Ralley was well-known among communities of retired veterans in the western contiguous states. She acted as the primary organizer and planner for all the regular reunions and get-togethers, and was always found willing to lead the regional committees as organized by the American Legion and Chamber of Commerce.

The Colonel was a proponent of strict, top-down hierarchy in all matters. Now that she was retired as *nearly* the first female commanding officer of a combat squadron, she endeavored to keep this same degree of military discipline in all aspects of her civilian life. Before her arrival at the Institute, the environment had lacked rigor. There had been invitees misplaced during their introductory tours, banquets where no vegan option had been on offer. The Sage took a liking to Colonel Ralley's way of doing things right away, and the Colonel was assigned to numerous Institute committees where she wasted no time in making her strong opinions known.

In her youth, Mike Ralley had been beautiful and blonde, yet austere. A firm jawline and a heavy brow gave her the natural appearance of a soldier. She was small, wiry, athletic and witty. She had limited family connections—and for this reason among others—was exactly the type of recruit that tends to make their way into special forces of one form or another.

Then there were always the rumors of androgyny, which helped to keep Mike at a distance from contemporaries, and propelled her into still higher ranks. In fact, it was widely speculated that Colonel Ralley's sexual features may have played a role in her unique special forces assignments. Whenever rarely concerns regarding the nature of this bias bubbled up to superiors, the military hierarchy declined to undermine on the basis of rumors alone. "The work speaks for itself," they would say, "and she's damn good at what she does."

Mickey Ralley never disappointed the Sage and never failed to tell her origin story for any guests who might listen:

She was born in Quebec and was abandoned by her parents as a young child, perhaps, some speculate, as a result of her non-conforming anatomical features. The Colonel crossed the border on her own, God knows how, and then, to survive, as she told it, ran a successful gang of street youths in Baltimore.

Young Mickey was collected by the police more than once, and was finally placed into foster care by human services when she was eleven. She enlisted the day she turned eighteen, and would have done so sooner were it not that she was caught by the recruiters trying to fake her age. She earned one degree on the Montgomery GI Bill between her tours of duty, then still others funded by grants and competitive scholarships. She made the jump to officer more swiftly than most, and served as a faculty member at the most prestigious military academies for over ten years, teaching *Just War Theory* and other, more eso-teric classes on leadership and organizational structure. During semester breaks, she was sent numerous times on international peacekeeping missions as a non-partisan observer for NATO, primarily in the Baltic States and Middle East. For these efforts and her otherwise extraordinary service, a graduation award at one academy had been named in her honor.

As a result of her disabilities, Colonel Mike Ralley was now bound by a chair. The marriage to Krystal Davis had been a stopgap measure in an otherwise downward trajectory of physical well-being. Krystal provided the Colonel stabil-ity and peace of mind—someone to care for her body when she could no longer manage to do so on her own, someone there for when the basic faculties of life continued to fail, one by one. Even so, the Colonel's voice remained authoritative; it came from a fortress of iron somewhere deep down within the hunched little woman.

And so it was often said that the greatest wisdom of the Sage was evident in her capacity for understanding the unique dispositions and intentions of others. This was her superpower, if indeed some sages have them. How exactly the Colonel came to be invited to the Institute, no one other than the Sage knew. Most of the administrators and staff assumed the Colonel's arrival was either directly or discreetly pursuant to her back-ground of distinguished service.

There had been grumblings that the appointment of the Colonel must surely be an anachronism. The Colonel had long ago lost her signature touch, some longstanding members of the Institute wrongly assumed. *"Sure she's highly-decorated, but she's been at a desk for all those years, and how long now has she been retired?"* But within a week of her arrival, those who had been foolish enough to speak such ill against little Mickey Ralley had been deftly silenced. In that first week, the Colonel both dissolved the Evaluation Review Committee and ocrapped an initiative to propose a state-level maritime forc Within no time, she had co-opted the authority of the Sage as her own, and used it to dominate the forward-facing machinery of the organization.

Thirteen

$\mathcal{T}$he ocean along Highway 1 was stretched taut like canvas, all the way out to the horizon. The sea was calm, but a large congregation of surfers waited for the two and sometimes three breaks at the national beach anyway. The date palms lining the path from the highway were laden with winter fruit. A few sticky dates fell here and there in the finely manicured turf.

Beyond an ivy wall lay Building Five, the living quarters for the most senior members of the Institute. In these sleek apartments, soft wood tones met the modern neutrals of the design features. The lighting adjusted automatically to the tone of conversation. Plush, but stark Norwegian-modernist furniture dotted the sitting rooms and the hallways.

Krystal Davis and her wife, Colonel Mickey "Mike" Ralley, sat together beside their oceanview window.

"Shall we take a Manhattan, Krystal dear?"

"That sounds like a wonderful idea, Mike. Let me just go fix it."

~

Krystal had at first been dumbstruck by the Colonel's forward sort of affection. They had met only once at the Soldiers' Center when the Colonel had abruptly proposed marriage.

Krystal admired the authoritative tone in Colonel Ralley's voice. She enjoyed listening to the Colonel's stories of war and lost, crazy adventure. Later, she was impressed by Mike's museum-quality collection of treasures shipped home via US Post from her many remote postings abroad. Communication hadn't always flowed easily, but now that Krystal Davis' Institute indoctrination was complete, conversation flowed more smoothly.

"The invitee Weaver has confirmed for next Tuesday," Krystal returned to the oceanside window with two, full coupe glasses. She placed the one with a straw in front of Colonel Mike Ralley on a tray.

"Excellent," said the Colonel. "Have our intentions advanced accordingly?"

A profile photo of Zora Weaver was displayed on the wall. Krystal then brought up the same photo for the Colonel on an electronic device next to the drink on the tray.

~

The two reviewed a Zora Weaver dressed in athletically form-fitting attire. In the photo, the young woman's head was tilted and she was laughing. The blonde-tipped coils of her hair leapt with potential energy against her honey-cinnamon skin.

"Oh Krystal, she's perfect. Activities please?"

"Near-Asian antiquities, massage, then golf."

"And she fits the characteristics?"

"Of course."

"Did you give her Jorge for the massage?"

"Yes, Mike. *Only the best this time.*"

"How about the invitee's next consultation?"

"She's selected surfing; a private cabana at the grottoes; and, if I'm not mistaken, she would appreciate a meal at *View of the Bluffs.*"

"Interested in the restaurant, is she?"

"Yes, I believe so. A special order has also been placed with the tailoring department."

Krystal adjusted the straw in Colonel Mike's drink before raising it to her wife's trembling mouth. She said: "I will ensure Zora continues to receive the very best treatment the Institute has to offer: Heladia for surfing instruction; her favorite snacks and drinks stocked at the cabana. I'll also check in with the chef about the menu for next Tuesday at *View of the Bluffs.*"

"Yes, let's do all of that. We need to keep this one, Krystal."

~

That weekend Krystal Davis set about the grounds to ensure all of the various amenities were in healthy condition. The infinity pool and grottoes were sparkling. The most in-demand cabana was reserved. Krystal checked the status of the work on the Crest Trail Loop, where workers were in the throes of repairing damage caused by a sinkhole. Beyond that, the far side of the lagoon was serving its purpose as a protected habitat for amberjack and plovers; on the near side, Institute members trained in outrigger canoes or sipped daquiris whilst walking the shell-littered shore.

The Events Center was booked out solid for private events; while at the beach, the sun was shining, the surf was high, and the kite surfing and other water sports were all highly afloat. Krystal made personally sure that the Special of the Day at *View of the Bluffs* the following Tuesday would be set as wild, fresh salmon, flown in from the Pacific Northwest, prepared with a side of fresh risotto. And so, by the end of her long inspection, Krystal Davis was confident that the Institute would provide Zora Weaver nothing but the most shining experience. Zora's dossier was updated and Krystal prepared a formal presentation.

Fourteen

The remembrance ceremony was set for the following Tuesday afternoon. As it happened, this was the time when the yoga studio could be made available and when the majority of the girls were not in class.

❧

Flowers had been delivered in great quantity; from the wood paneling of the walls rebounded and reverberated the warm and enchanting fragrance. Presenting the flowers in the shape of a young woman assuming the *Baddha Konasana* pose, as had been originally planned, had been scrapped as tasteless. The floral assault organized to summit the original endeavor had to be repurposed last-minute, and the yoga studio was now so replete with floral arrangements in all corners that all ancillary features of the room had to be moved aside in order to accommodate.

One of the Littles stood to prepare the music for the ceremony in an area usually reserved for seating cushions, now also the temporary home of shunted-aside rowing machines, yoga wedges and foam rollers. A muffled, indefinite tension was palpable, like a large ship slipping past the craggy coast-line in the dark. The smart speakers were connected, the sound experience was customizable. Devotional music was tested at varying levels of decibel. The heat from the lighting prompted greatly expedited respiration from the collection of flowers so assembled, the force of this aroma laying waste, in the end, to the tension, the noise, and the heat.

≈

The move away from the anthropomorphic floral arrangement had led some earmarked funds to be transferred to the social committee, now tasked with managing the food and beverage for both the ceremony itself, and for any planned or unplanned after-parties. The result of this unfortunate turn of events, at long end, was to commission a multilayer cake, a particular fad of that moment across internet pinboards, carved to represent a venerational bust of their dearly departed sister.

Discounting the lovely fondant blossom exquisitely tucked into its ganache and butter cream shroud, the result-ing gâteau was as hideous as it was grotesque. Thick and heavy sugar paste hair parted at the crown of the skull to reveal the scalp, painted in the same shade of delicate pink as the whites of the eyes and gums. Weiwei's teeth of coated resin and wax shone to illustrate, perhaps for the benefit of the artist alone, the care by which they had been placed in their sockets with such precision.

~

"Well, what do you think?" Whispered MacKenzie reverentially, as if Weiwei herself might be listening from the great beyond.

The torso of the custom cake, constructed from oblong bricks of crisped rice and marshmallow, was melting. Weiwei's dull eyes sang pleadingly toward the heat of the lights.

MacKenzie stood firmly beside the atrocity in defiance, now too immersed in colloquium to devise a political exit. "So, what do you think?" She asked Zora again.

"It's quite striking—unmistakably her."

"*I know, right?*"

"How are you planning to slice it?"

"Let's not worry about that just yet. That's one detail I have no concern, the alcohol will help us to sort out."

Fifteen

*E*nergy was high in the yoga studio that afternoon. Several freshmen not yet Health and Wellness members, but who had already expressed a strong interest, served the mimosas and box wine. The social buzz galvanized into a sustained murmur and from there into a rotary hum as the conversations piqued and the alcohol began to take hold.

MacKenzie, as was customary, stood at the center of it all:

"Zora, sweetheart, some of the members of the social committee had an idea about what to do with the cake. *Have you tried any yet?*"

"I've been waiting for the others to try it first."

"*Yes,* well, between the calories and the ingredient list, I'm sure we'll have a fair amount left over. God forbid these girls forsake a mimosa for a slice or two of cake. *Also,* did you know that the whole frame of that thing is held together with shortening? *So gross!* If word gets around about that, I doubt anyone will touch any *at all*."

"What a shame—"

"Yes. I completely agree. Such a waste of funds. To make up for it, some of the others and I have decided to further honor Weiwei by interring the bust—or whatever portion remains after the ceremony today and any after-parties—at sea. Someone said that Weiwei always loved the ocean. Plus, we can get all dressed up and take pictures for the house webpage. *Let's be honest*, organizational recruiting being what is it these days, we can't stand to wait too long. Thank you, by the way, for sending that speech."

"Of course. Did you like it?"

"I haven't read it yet. I'm sure it's wonderful, though, *so thanks so much for that*. By the way, your name came up at our last board meeting. Sophia Buonanni even said, 'Poor Zora. She must be taking all of this *so hard*. The best thing we can do for her is probably to keep her busy.'

"We've decided to inter the cake at Panther Beach. It's easy enough to get to, and the rocks and cliffs should make it convenient to drop poor Weiwei right in. I can take the cake and a couple of the girls to help make sure it doesn't topple over in the back of my Mercedes. Would you be a doll and look into flexible bus fares for yourself and twelve or fifteen of the other girls? I know you're an expert at taking that route."

～

Zora did not wait to hear MacKenzie read the remembrance that afternoon. It was all just too sickening, with everyone angling for Weiwei to be remembered in their own particular way.

Zora used the darkening of the room during the slide-show as an opportunity to slip out the side door. Her appointment at the Institute was set for that evening. She boarded the public bus just as the sun began its nightly plunge toward the ocean.

Part Two

Sixteen

It reminded Zora of stock photos she'd seen of the
Pantheon in Rome. A sweeping staircase tiled in white
and blue led into a complex of seemingly ancient structures.
The remaining sun of the day peeked in through the breezeways. A sloping ramp of tempered shale led still further, *up
and up.*

Other than light seeping in from the oculus, the space
Zora entered was dark. A color projection ran before her on
the wall; she stopped and was at once immersed in the colossal,
projected imagery.

The voice in the recording was the same voice from
countless product commercials, feminine and authoritative:

> *Welcome to the Temple of Minerva-
> by-the-Sea at View of the Bluffs, where for
> three-quarters of a century, the exceptional
> have come to cultivate their best selves.*
>
> *Institute facilities are equipped with the
> most modern in climate control and air filtra-
> tion systems. Please note the exquisite grade*

of material used in the construction of our campus. Each component material has been selected as representative of the highest quality: Calacatta marble imported from Tuscany, glass masterworks designed by Chihuly himself.

Our unparalleled botanical collection encompasses rare and exotic species from across six continents. Of particular note are our extensive fruit orchards, enhanced by seeds acquired from around by the world by the Sage herself while serving on diplomatic and good-will missions.

Zora listened, feeling vaguely captive, smothered by the surety in the ethereal, recorded voice. The spell was as captivating as any spell might be. Then there was a pause, and, *"Welcome to the Temple of Minerva-by-the-Sea—"* the loop began again.

Zora found a console on the wall and used it to stop the recording altogether. In its absence, the rotunda was transformed into a soft place of solemn reflection, a simple, gray chamber. A hostess leading an awestruck young couple stepped in through a wall of artisanal, edible greens.

"What you see here is our Temple to Minerva *slash* Waiting Area," she announced. "Please follow me. We have a private table already prepared. *Right this way, please."* The couple was entirely engaged in the moment. As if two were one, they appeared cornered in the initial spasms of love or any other lustful enterprise.

The host touched the opposite wall of artisanal, edible greens and the congregation stepped through. Zora waited several minutes for them to clear out before following.

~

In opposition to the austere confines of the temple, what lay beyond seemed of a different world. Here native agave met banana and date palms, San Pedro sentries kept armies of jasmine and tuberose at bay. Several front-facing tables lay just beyond a pristine moat. Each was separated from the others by elaborate walls of topiary. Every table offered unfettered views of the water, including the volcano island that erupted with a bubble lightshow once every fifteen minutes during regular dining hours. On Zora's side of the moat, nearest the Victorian Orangerie, small golden plaques made up a part of a decorative wall. These plaques recorded the Institute's principal family donors from New York and Silicon Valley.

~

The cool and the stillness brought by the onset of evening began to settle in on the lawns. Stage lighting and illuminated pathways took the place of natural sunlight. Zora followed an exposed, natural ridgeline to a well-manicured patch of Bermuda grass. At the center of this lawn was a stone monument where the Sage had been honored with a plaque making note of her several, generous donations.

A symphony of waves roared down below. And there was Highway 1, its long worm of headlights and taillights easing its way, all the way back to the hotels and restaurants of Santa Cruz.

Zora sat in a bed of ice plant with her notebook and her pens. Before the Institute, writing had to be squeezed in, between class and exercise and social demands. Precious moments of privacy were too oft quashed by meddlesome priers. So Zora huddled outside, writing in secret, hoping that one day she would at once be able to say it the way it had to be said.

She wrote:

> Weiwei dearie no one knew
>
> One little thing about you
>
> I remember nothing yet
>
> Others still I can't forget;
>
> To atone we baked a cake,
>
> Promptly forgotten at your wake.

Perhaps this night was not one for striving, Zora thought as she read the words back. She looked out on the ocean, the all-powerful archetype for birth and death—and now, suddenly, the metaphor for Weiwei Li, as ordained by MacKenzie Benoit.

Poor Weiwei thought Zora, *they didn't even get that right.*

~

The night surfers were out. With headlights strapped to their caps, these phosphorescent athletes swung together in the darkness, crossing paths.

Zora heard a voice calling to her from beyond the curtain of wavesound. It was the voice which said nothing but quelled all thought. Now was the time to watch the planets and the indistinct stars as they appeared, one by one—allowing the pinks, the oranges, and the yellows to blur together into a deep cosmic blue.

Seventeen

Of all the restaurants in a thousand restaurant dreams, this was the one. *View of the Bluffs* did nothing if not resound with the immense sparkle of glamour. It was built along the long spine of the mountain in contour with the natural shape of the ridge. The dining chamber came appointed with both a parlor and a lounge, and these rooms jutted out from the main dining area at the austere angles of the mountain.

Directly below the table, Hole Eighteen of *The Bluffs* was lit by the moon. At this hour, the golfers were gone, and the course on the bluffs lay dormant in hues of cool, muted blue.

The window across the way in the parlor was even more enthralling. It faced the heights of the gardens, where white tigers prowled the boulders just behind glass. Beyond that and far below, the night surfers rode up and over the crests like electric rodeo, carving the coastline and dancing on foam.

"You must be hungry," Krystal Davis handed Zora a glass of champagne. "I'm so sorry I'm late. Time sometimes gets away from us here at the Institute. Thank you in advance for your kind understanding."

"It's no trouble. This is an absolutely beautiful spot and I was just doing some writing, actually."

"For Weiwei's remembrance?"

"Oh no, that's all over now, thank you. And I'm sorry, but I guess I won't be needing any of the tailoring after all. I really am terribly sorry for any inconvenience I may have caused you or the Sage of the tailoring department."

Krystal never wasted an opportunity. Her pupils grew large. "No need to worry," she said. "We'll figure something out," and, after a moment more, "Did you say you were writing?"

"Yes—well, I'm trying."

"You're the second real writer I've ever met, *after the Sage, that is.*" Her eyebrow raised: "What are you writing?"

"Philosophy, I think."

"Just like the Sage."

"I'm not sure you could say that, exactly."

"Have you studied her works?"

"I wasn't aware she had any works."

"The literary works of the Sage are not for everybody and that's why we don't evangelize broadly. Some time ago, another girl from the university got quite lost in the idea of it all. It's a tragic story, really, and I'm afraid she's no longer with us."

"What does that mean? *Lost in the idea of it all?* And what makes you think I'll be able to handle it any better?"

"I wouldn't be here if I gave up the Institute's secrets so easily, Ms. Weaver."

"It does seem like an interesting job," Zora conceded.

Krystal Davis' response came strictly from the manual:

"The Institute is my greatest connection to the world. Without it, I'd be lost in a maelstrom of self-doubt and unrecognized potential. When I reside here, I needn't *work*. I *volunteer* to serve the purpose with my gifts—*to make life better for us all over time*—according to the will of the almighty Sage. I and many others would welcome a young philosopher like you to our esteemed ranks, Zora. *Who knows?* Maybe you will write something to be read in tens of thousands of years. My own thinking will never be of that caliber, but the great works of the Sage, *and maybe of you*—well, who is to say what will be saved for posterity? I could never do what you do. I could never leave traces of my imperfect work—with everything being so discoverable these days—"

"Is that what you worry about?"

"Yes, of course. Don't you? The only thing I know in this life, is that you can't trust anybody about anything."

"That's sad. *You can't possibly think that—*"

"*I do and do you really want to know why?* I'll tell you but only because you're a philosopher like the Sage and maybe it'll do some good in this world for you in particular to know. It's kind of a long story."

∽

"My lifestyle is what you might call fluid. I grew up poor in Milwaukee in the 1980s when Daddy and Mommy were hooked on crack cocaine. That's tough for a kid, you know, and I don't remember much of it.

"If you asked me what year something happened or what grade I was in, I couldn't tell you. We didn't have birthdays to celebrate, and when Daddy *was* around, he'd just call us by our number in the order we came out. To him, I was always number three, because I had two older sisters.

"I got married as soon as I could and had kids—two of them. I worked as a Navy medic for a while and everything was going normal. But, *you know*, I always had this itch. I don't know if you've ever felt an itch like this before, but it grabbed ahold of me and wouldn't let go."

"Then what happened?"

"I got a divorce and got out of the Navy. I lived in a cabin in Virginia for a while—rekindled a few romances put on hold by my first marriage. Then I got sick of the weather and the politics and moved to sunny California.

"In California I used my expertise from the Navy to find work as a medical device salesperson—but the California taxes *are terrible*, so I cashed out on my house and moved to Las Vegas.

"I was working conventions—for the money and also to meet new people—when a mutual friend introduced me to Colonel Mike."

"That's interesting."

"The Colonel is a proud woman. That's one thing about her—she doesn't ever want to let on when she knows she's licked.

"Before she moved in here—*into the Institute*—she lived in a house in Las Vegas where it was convenient for her to get the treatment she needed.

"The house was amazing—completely rigged for her to get about on her own—in spite of her disabilities—which were already serious by that time. Then she started falling over. At first, I was recommended to her for my medical training, but the Colonel also appreciated my military experience and the fact I had no trouble understanding the military mindset.

"Before now I never really had a stable place. I mean, when I was married, *yes—but he beat me*—not all the time, but enough to make me want to just get away. Plus, I was *so lonely*. You're still young so you couldn't possibly understand—all that moving around, all that loss that just comes with living a life and getting old, trying to do good or at least not do too badly. It changes someone and there's not much one can do about it." Krystal caught her breath before adding: "The Colonel offered me stability. That's why I'm here."

"But you love the Colonel?"

To this Krystal did not immediately respond. Her eyes welled with loss and self-pity. Then she spoke:

"Some of the gals I met in Vegas suggested I get in touch with Colonel Mike; that's how it happened. So I did and do you know what? Colonel Mike has the most interesting stories. I liked that about her right away and she has lots of stories to tell. Now that we live at the Institute, the Colonel doesn't need me as much or in the same ways any more. Now there is one porter to change her and two to lift her up, one to bathe her and a nurse to distribute her medications every day at six and noon. Physical therapy is at one PM after lunch. Not to mention all the regular activities to which the Colonel and I enjoy executive access."

"I guess you must be feeling a bit like you've lost your role?"

"That's exactly right, I guess. You must really be a good philosopher, Zora. I have *too much* here at the Institute and I'm *too old* to start over again. But I am lonely. Having all this and no one to share it with is another kind of misery altogether."

"Do you regret getting married?"

"Oh Lord, no! Everybody gets lonely sometimes. No matter what happens, I have the resources of the Colonel behind me. My official duty as a wife remains seeing to the Colonel's fitness and well-being."

"And it sounds like what you have here is better than anything you've ever had before?"

"Yes—but it's so much more than that."

"What do you mean?"

"The Sage insists that we look presentable, stay fit, and cultivate our minds. I know this can all sound like a bunch of hocus pocus, but to really do this, *to be this,* all of the time—it's all-consuming. I serve only at the pleasure of the Sage and the Colonel and this is my reward—spending time with impressive young women and men and introducing them to our secret of success. Search yourself and answer: *Why did you come here?*"

"I was searching for something."

"Without the teachings of the Sage and the direction of the Colonel, I would have never found my place in this world. Now that I'm here and I've found it, I feel ever more at peace. I'm no philosopher, but that must count for something."

"So it's peace you're after?" Zora asked.

"Yes, that and serving the aims of the Institute. And finding my own way—"

"...*Neither my joy nor my sorrow can satisfy me...*"

"Say that again."

"...*Neither my joy nor my sorrow can satisfy me—I am the thirst; I am the worst—but a line of skulls has brought me here. This thought devours me.*"

"Yes, that's wonderful. Is there any more?"

"Much more. It's from one of my favorite books of philosophy, *Heroes for All Time*, by Mariko Nakagawa."

A bottle of champagne arrived at the table. One of the tigers pawed at the glass in the parlor. Krystal tasted the champagne, then nodded to the waiter for a long pour, "I think you'll fit in perfectly, Zora, reading your books and writing your philosophy up here with us on the bluffs.

Eighteen

K rystal Davis was methodical in all of her undertakings. She stalked her prey like Lady Minna Jenkins summitting the wintry passes of Ladakh. The next morning in the Orangerie, she set to cutting the roses just as they had surpassed peak hydration levels. A hand pruner was provided by an assistant, and a container filled with cool water was made ready to immerse the cut stems. With slow but steady movements, Krystal chose the best buds—those strengthened by the sun but not yet fully open. She tended to several of the pristine bushes as a barber would so many customers, snipping at the longest and most sinewed of the stems. One by one, each severed masterpiece was dropped into its cool bath.

When Krystal's concentration took her far afield of the collecting container, the assistant scurried back and forth to make deposits. Each exquisite creation was held as if the delicate stem might shatter were it exposed to even the slightest unpleasance. No one at the Institute was Krystal's equal in tending to the roses. No one else even came close.

～

It was of course usual at the residences of Health and Wellness, for gifts from admirers to stream in—chocolates, jewelry items, perfumes, ready-to-order bouquets; each girl tended to her own. It was perhaps well then that Zora lived a relatively cloistered existence in the Susan E. Gephardt College Apartments. Whereas the Health and Wellness house remained a constant beehive of activity and chatter, the Susan E. Gephardt College Apartments might as well have been Antarctica. As it happened, only MacKenzie was present to be fiendishly jealous when the package from Krystal Davis was delivered by private courier—

—not that Zora was entirely comfortable with a gift of fifty long stem roses in gilded boxes with tissue paper packed so exquisitely as to discourage even their unwrapping. The message seemed clear. From seed to scent, the oeuvre of romance was in this gesture.

"You slut!" MacKenzie laughed. "I've never known you to give it up so easily. Good for you, girl." Then, after a momentary pause, "That must have been some really good champagne they gave you," and then, "Hey, what's in the envelope?"

Zora hadn't yet considered it. MacKenzie grabbed for the gift playfully. Then, all elbows and brute, feminine strength, MacKenzie boxed the other girl out as she plucked the embossed envelope from the boxes to open and read aloud:

Dear Ms. Weaver,

We hope you enjoyed your recent visit to the Institute. This card entitles you to the following amenities to help you make continued use of our services in your search to find the ideal you:

✓ *One tailored wetsuit*

✓ *Six private surfing lessons with Heladia, the Institute's surfing pro*

✓ *Three months' access to the private beach cabana*

✓ *$600 in credit at the beach cabana bar*

Please feel free to contact the reservations department at your convenience to book your services.

Warmly,

Krystal Davis

In spite of how even more jealous these added offerings made MacKenzie Benoit, this all seemed like rather *a lot* to Zora, and she knew better than to trust her emotional well-being to University Counselling Services.

Zora had, upon her arrival the previous autumn, invested in a psychological well-being subscription service for times of acute emotional distress. HelpSpace catered to Zora's demographic exactly: using the convenient application platform, the customer sends a text chat to the care team, which offers the patient real-time support and therapeutic services. So far, Zora had used HelpSpace to call on advice before major exam dates, and on one time in particular, when a *Legal Studies* exam fell on the same day as a *Technology of Third World Countries* presentation and a Health and Wellness rush event.

That had all been before the internship and poor Weiwei's untimely demise, *long ago*, when curricular issues such as exams seemed like a big deal.

Now, suddenly, everything was happening at a pace Zora couldn't manage on her own. It was too cold and gusty outside to sit in the gardens under the Banksias. Behind the closed door of her apartment room, Zora texted in chat:

> *Hi,*
>
> *In case my files aren't up-to-date I want to first remind you that I am a college student with testing anxiety but no other diagnosed illnesses. You may be able to see in your system that my last text was two weeks ago about an unusual invitation I had received. Just in case, I wanted to remind you that I accepted the invitation and was introduced to the most wonderful place called the Institute. It really is a great privilege and an honor to be associated with this place in any way, and they've invited me to keep attending as a guest.*
>
> *There is a woman there who is quite impressive. In several overt ways, she has made*

it clear that her reason for inviting me is roman-
tically motivated. She is married, but this mar-
riage is one of convenience, and I don't think it
would be a problem for her to keep other con-
current relationships. In fact, she told me quite
directly she has done as much in the past. She is
much older than I ···· I ·l· ··· ····· ··· ····
feelings for her as I do for attractive, younger
classmates I see at the gym or in class, but I do
feel a strong respect for her accomplishments
and want to learn more.

Yet I am conflicted. I feel there are a num-
ber of peculiarities concerning her advances
and the Institute's motives that may put their
offer at odds with my personal philosophy and
better judgement.

First, there is the issue about her being
married, which I believe I have already
explained. She also seems to be using her sta-
tus and access as a means to pursue me. This
is more than flattering, of course, but I'm not
sure if someone should be abusing their offi-
cial capacity in this way, especially over me.
Again, she's shared her intentions with me in
quite straightforward ways, so I feel certain
this is the case and that I'm not misinterpret-
ing. What's more is that this tendency for her to
be straightforward is something I respect and
something I do find subtly attractive.

Then there is also the question about the organization this woman represents. I have only had a few interactions there so far, but I feel certain that my personal philosophy is not in alignment with the underlying philosophy of this place. I must say, I am undergoing a sort of a metamorphosis in my personal development at present. I can be rash in decision-making, and, because of that, I'm unduly susceptible to outside influence. I wouldn't want the philosophy of The Institute and of these women to somehow corrupt my personal beliefs or works.

On the other hand, the facilities and opportunities I am being offered at the Institute seem unparalleled, and the purpose, they tell me, is exactly that of perfecting my own personal efforts.

I hope you may be starting to see why I feel so conflicted.

The woman who invited me has a distinguished look and the most amazing hair. Under normal circumstances, without a conscience clouded by all these lingering details, I might date her; but for right now, I'm just not sure.

Thank you in advance for your reply, and I'm sorry this request is so long.

Nineteen

The main customer interface of HelpSpace was several masters and doctorate-level professionals from the less-distinguished universities of the Northeast. The diplomas hanging on their cubicle partitions were professionally printed to exacting standards, but they *were not* written in Latin, nor did they display any ribbon adornment as sometimes do the diplomas of more upscale institutions. And while the medical doctors to which the HelpSpace customer service representatives sometimes made referrals were free to work from home, the service associate team shared a small, windowless room in a business park in the suburbs outside Philadelphia.

Sarita Reddy had, against the most fervent wishes of her parents, pursued a masters of social work. She was now uninterestingly mired in the throes of a mid-career layover. Years ago, romantic and impressionable Sarita had begun her service career as a bureaucrat in the state offices. She transitioned to the local health system when the pay had proved a modicum better. Sarita was new to HelpSpace; she secretly hoped it would be the hinge position to swing her into the much more lucrative world of *tech*.

From the hours of eight AM to five PM every Monday through Friday, Sarita shared a double-wide cubicle with Ted Nelson, Jr. Each associate sat with their back facing the other, toward their computer monitors and the outer walls.

"*Dear Zora,*" Sarita Reddy started to type as she released a long, pleading sigh, "*I am to some extent concerned by the rapid changes in your emotional state.*"

The cough and cold lozenges Sarita had been consuming were advertised to provide *a cool breath of relief.* Yet even now she sniffled and wretched in the room without windows—and all through the long winter snows, Ted Nelson, Jr. had borne the discomfort along with her.

Ted often took to earbuds if and when Sarita's phlegm-soaked chorus grew too much to bear. Recently he thought maybe she was back on the road to health. But today again seemed to Ted like something of a setback. Sarita coughed, gasped, and snorted as she spoke aloud, typing again:

> *Deciding between idealism and security is a time-honored rite of passage in societies throughout the world. The nervousness that often accompanies such life-stage transitions is entirely natural. Don't feel guilty about your own success! Proceed with caution, but proceed optimistically. Someday you will look back on the trials of your youth from a position of security. Surely it is the highest endeavor of woman to extend the human vision toward progress and into the future.*

As for your personal convictions, the ide-
alism and passion you feel now will fade with
time. As with any decision on the path of life, it
is important to leave it to your own best judge-
ment to help you decide.

Sarita Reddy read the last bit aloud to Ted, then asked: "Is that too direct?"

"Most of it is pretty direct, Sarita."

"—*Ugh*. I can't seem to get over this cold. My throat is all scratchy. We get a few requests like this at the beginning of every college semester: '*Help me, I'm not sure what I want to do with my life*,' you know, that sort of thing."

"We do get '*em*."

"Maybe I'll try for something slightly more toned down. The next one in my queue is a pornography addiction. What did you say to the last one of those?"

"I told him meditation and cold showers."

"Right, meditation. That's the part I forgot."

∾

Across the country in sunny California, Zora's alone time was interrupted by disturbing news from the balcony. The window for interring Weiwei's bust, or the portion that remained, was something demanding of Zora's attention. All that was left of the artful creation was a portion of the lower left ear, the chin, the neck, and some of the hair. According to MacKenzie, most of the face had been eaten when Hannah Morgan shared the original creation with her fitness center class. A late evening after a swim team party accounted for the destruction—*one way or another*—of most of the rest. The horrific contortion now slumped on its back in a part of the cake box used in its original delivery.

Poor Weiwei no longer had eyes to see nor a mouth to taste, but if she had, she would have found herself stale in some places and starting to turn in others. A blessed thing was that it was winter, so the flies and other small insects that may have been attracted by such a sweet feast were not of major concern.

"We're planning a trip to Panther Beach to get rid of this thing," MacKenzie reminded Zora. "Don't forget to get the bus tickets. Here's the petty cash and make sure you get a receipt."

Zora accepted, but her attention remained transfixed on the grisly remnants of her suitemate in the box on the table.

"Here," said MacKenzie, handing Zora a Solo cup half-full of chardonnay, "you'll need this." Then she added with a snort, "Once we get rid of this cake, this nightmare will all be over."

～

Timing and luck may well be the most important factors in living a good life, and fortunately for Zora, an amazing thing happened. An electric truck with tinted windows made its way up the university drive, dodging cyclists and pedestrians. At that precise moment, Zora received a text:

> *Look down. See the car. The limousine service is here for you, Zora.*

"Who is this?" Zora texted back.

The door of the vehicle popped open and a customer service associate wearing a white satin uniform stepped out. He opened the rear door of the truck and then stepped aside.

"It looks like they're here for you," MacKenzie offered.

"Yeah, I guess I'll see you later. Will you finish my wine?"

~

At the national beach, the native Californians were bundled against the cold. Tourists hid behind dark glasses, anxiously awaiting the sun God's return. There was somewhat less of a frenzy than usual for the first-come, first-serve parking spaces at the national beach along Highway 1. A crisp gale blew in from the west and north; it licked at sweatshirts clinging forlornly to elbows.

Zora watched in silence from behind the tinted windows of the luxury vehicle. She would dine with the Colonel Mike Ralley and Krystal tonight. This was all she had been told.

In fact, Zora wasn't at all prepared for dinner, and she had made this clear by protesting the plans slightly. The driver made quick assurances that the Institute's full slate of spa services and amenities would be available for use upon arrival, should Zora need to freshen up.

"But I'm only wearing my yoga clothes," Zora protested again.

"Your formal evening wear has been made available by the tailor, Ms. Weaver. Bespoke garments await you at the spa."

Twenty

The Colonel was a hunched, little woman with silver hair who wore tailored athletic suits. That afternoon, the orderlies had worked together to lift her frail body—one growing more and more rigid, day by day, month by month. They changed her undergarments and gave her a sponge bath. Then they attired her in her newest and most crisp set of leisure wear. To her jacket was affixed official insignia and a rainbow's worth of decoration. She said:

"It seems you have made an impression on our recruitment committee. Especially on my wife who—*I might add*—also happens to serve as committee chair."

"Thank you both for your support and encouragement."

"I even mentioned you to the Sage herself, you should know."

"I'm speechless. It's truly such an honor just to be here."

The restaurant tigers were not on display and when Zora remarked as to their absence, the lure of a live peacock was ushered into the enclosure on the other side of the glass.

"Ms. Weaver, here at the Institute we like to think of ourselves as a forward-thinking organization. The Sage's most profound thought centers on the future, and specifically on what we can all do to ensure the best possible future for all of human society and the world.

"In accordance with this mission, the Sage has ordained that the time has come when the underrepresented are recognized and incorporated equitably into all echelons of our increasingly fragile society.

"Take Krystal as a model; though her background and personality characteristics are not exactly the same as yours— we need more valued members like her and like you.

"This is exactly why the Sage has placed a freeze on Institute membership for the next several cycles, except in cases such as yours where the extending of an invitation would enhance the Institute's diversity profile."

"I see."

"No need to thank us now. The honor is ours; I can assure you. May I inform the Sage that you have accepted?"

"I'm grateful for the opportunity, I'm sure."

"In addition to joining as a full member—*because this has also been approved*—it has been requested that you embark upon your service journey here by chairing a committee. This will be under Krystal's guidance, of course, and the aim would be to look into some of these particular hot-button issues and reimagine how we could improve our recruitment strategies."

"It sounds like such an honor. What's the name of the committee?"

"Oh, I'm not certain. Krystal, do we have a name?"

"*Diversity and Membership Equity*—or maybe *Societal Equity and the Underprivileged*—I can't remember exactly right now—we'll probably have to look it up."

"It doesn't matter, Zora," continued the Colonel as the drinks arrived. "I'll tell you what—*you name the committee. Name it whatever you'd like. Treat it as a first order of business. It's your committee now."

～

Once all this lofty talk had died down, Zora excused herself to visit the powder room. This was a luxurious space. The dim ambiance was accentuated by recessed accent lighting. Fresh cloth hand towels were available in abundance instead of their paper counterpart. Particularly impressive among the individually-wrapped toiletries were the single-use dental floss kits, of which Zora took several. She inspected herself in the vanity mirror wearing her brand-new, thin-lapeled suit. With controlled and deliberate movements, Zora touched up the work of the professional cosmetologist. She read the label affixed to the Bemberg lining of her new attire: "*Handcrafted from the finest Italian fabric for Ms. Zora Weaver.*" It was signed: "*The Institute Tailors.*"

Next to the bathroom mirror, a porthole window exposed the layering of the clouds above the sea: orange, blue, gray, purple—each of the colors of the day outdid one another in one final face off with the dusk.

Twenty-one

*N*ow that the champagne was working its first effects, Zora took a moment to glance all around at the décor of the dining room. Potted ferns hung in baskets from exposed beams. A fan constructed from antique airplane propellers gyrated on the ceiling. Several opulent booths with plush, blue cushioning were sunk like jeweled islands in a midnight sea, dotting the archipelago between Zora, the bar, the grand piano, and her table. Soft, piped music resonated from the uppermost corners, and, from all the way up there, Zora heard a familiar tone. It was almost airy, with a nasal timbre.

"Professor Dinkelstein, may I have the pleasure of introducing Ms. Zora Weaver?"

The Professor rose to greet Zora. He did not seem to remember her from the Soldiers' Memorial Services Center, or at least he made no overt effort to show it if he did. After exchanging pleasantries, the two sat back down and smiled politely. It seemed to Zora she may have interrupted an important conversation:

"The question is what to do now with the grass-roots level of our outreach," continued the Colonel with the apparent topic. "If the packets and evaluations are of no use anymore except in a few specialized cases, is there a better way to invest the time we spend on these sessions? I don't know about you, but I am of the mind that we ought to say nothing, continue collecting data as we always have, and destroy all that we don't need—*which is almost everything*—as we have already been doing for some time now in accordance with our own internal standards. I recognize, however, that this course presents certain risks over time—*as all charted courses will*—and that some other esteemed members of the committee may disagree with my opinion on the matter."

∼

What first struck Zora about Professor Dinkelstein's appearance was his thinning hair, which was as wispy as his voice. She noted his top-heavy skull, poked in the center by wire-rimmed glasses. The Professor's skin was remarkably taught and unblemished for a man with such little hair. His eyes were greenish and alert. They focused resolutely on Zora across the table with unchanging expression.

"You see, Zora," the Professor went right into explaining, "We've learned so much from our session evaluations over the years, we simply no longer need to collect data from most demographic groups with which we engage. We know what we're looking for. And this something is very particular. It is from these groups alone, that we actually require *more data.*

The Colonel tells me you're going to be leading our committee to look into these and other issues, especially as they relate to future classes of Institute invitees," Professor Dinkelstein sat back in his chair.

"It's quite an honor to be invited and to be asked. It's all been so sudden—"

"It's merely a question of talent, Ms. Weaver. From what we've heard and inferred about you from your surveys and your volunteer work, it seems a proper fit. It's quite unusual to invite a new member to chair a committee in this way, I'm sure you understand."

"Professor Dinkelstein serves on the—*What was the name of your committee again, Professor Dinkelstein?*" Krystal asked.

"*The Committee for Liaising and…Liaising and Member—no, no, that's not it…*I'm afraid I can't remember at present."

"Whatever the name," Krystal continued, unruffled, "new committees such as yours will be considered as sub-committees of the Professor's overarching institutional committee, and your committee's work will ultimately be reviewed by the superseding committee and its membership, both voting members and *ex-officio.*"

"Zora," the Professor asked directly, now with a glint in his eye. "Would you do me the pleasure of meeting me for a game of squash later this week or next? We have the most wonderful squash facilities here at the Institute."

Zora hesitated. She had never played or even heard of squash. But before she could even think, the Colonel had accepted the Professor's invitation on her behalf.

~

In this and other matters, the evening did not turn out quite as Zora had hoped. Despite the undeniably impressive meal in the grandiose hall, Zora knew Dr. Dinkelstein only as a voice from the front of an empty room—as the leader of a cult, *maybe*—one which collected endless quantities of unused and un-useful personal data.

That night before Zora went to bed, she punched out a chat request to her designated HelpSpace representative.

Twenty-two

The studio was awash in post workout fury and scent—lavender and argan, magnolia and verbena—all merged as one in a delicate fog on the window panes. Caffeinated young women, on their second or third cups of chai, stood in groups and mingled, discussing what to wear to Panther Beach, and sourcing information for themselves about Weiwei.

"*Like*, these events can trigger all sorts of strange reactions in people. It really underscores the importance of, *like*, regular wellness checks."

"I know, I *like* totally agree, and I feel like grief and sadness are triggered in different ways for different people."

"*Yay!* We are so totally on the same wavelength about this."

"*I know, right?*"

And from another corner:

"I heard she went to Student Services but they weren't able to help."

"*I know.* The problem is that you don't just walk into Student Services and get service. You have to be tested and approved for service, and then they analyze your data and recommend a personal improvement plan. My roommate freshman year was registered with Student Services and attended some group sessions and clinics, so that's how I know."

~

MacKenzie directed all the action from the corner of the room. A kiss on the cheek here, a hug or two over there, expressions of joy and disbelief, all were tools at the ready for the sophomore representative to the Board. Had they been there to witness, none of her private tutors would have been surprised to watch MacKenzie revel glowingly in it all. As she caught sight of Zora through the curls and the groups of young women, MacKenzie trained her focus. She moved across the room like a cheetah hunts wildebeest on the plains of the Serengeti.

"Did you get the tickets?" She asked.

"What tickets?"

"The bus tickets. For tomorrow. *Remember*? We need twelve plus yours. *Thirteen total.* You took the petty cash."

"Oh, that's right. I'm so sorry about that. I still have the pretty cash and yes, I'll pick them up tomorrow morning before we go."

"Good," said MacKenzie, turning to the rest of the room, as would a maestro turn to ready the orchestra at the start of a symphony:

"*Ladies,*" she announced to get their attention. Then once more, "*Sisters, please.*"

The busy room slowed as the bustle softened to a muffle and then wound down. The ancillary conversations came to a stop altogether as all the fit bodies turned to their beautiful and composed leader.

"These have been a trying few days for our little community of like-minded members," remarked MacKenzie.

Several of the girls agreed from the crowd.

"It's been *tough*—with all of us experiencing this tragedy in our own ways—I know it's been painful for each of us—

"Tomorrow, we leave for Panther Beach at two PM to celebrate Weiwei's life. This should give us plenty of time for those wonderful portrait shots I know so many of you have been preparing. According to the weather reports, it's not going to be totally sunny, but please remember to apply sunscreen as needed. The social committee has purchased bottled water to bring along if anyone needs it—*unless they've already replaced it with rosé*—"

This quip received the chuckle it deserved and then the room once again settled into anticipatory silence.

"Zora will be paying for a group of you on the bus—*sorry about the public transportation, girls*—and Hannah, Emma and I will be bringing the supplies in my Mercedes."

"Poor Weiwei!" Someone yelled.

"We love you, Weiwei!" Someone else did.

"*Yes*. We all loved Weiwei in life and we miss her dearly. I can't even begin to imagine what it would be like for us to move forward individually or as a group without her. But *we must*. We are strong and strong Weiwei would have wanted it this way. *I love all of you*. Please come prepared to have fun as we share in Weiwei's memory. *Does anyone have any questions?*"

Twenty-three

For 100 million years from 130 to 30 million years ago, the California coast as we know it was thrust upward and out of the sea. So let not the traffic jams nor the strip malls fool you, the primal here is never very far away.

Jeweled coves. Ribbons of mountain. Those medicinal aromas of pine and eucalyptus. In the time of Zora Weaver, the ethereal sun still glistened twinkle steps across the water, showering all the people with that feeling of first love.

∾

The lavatory mirrors of H&W House were packed, shoulder to shoulder, elbow to elbow, with excitable girls in preparation for an event. After morning classes and tofu lunches, the sophomore class of Health and Wellness readied themselves for their long-awaited devotional excursion. Lantern sleeves and muffy legwarmers were that season's style; everyone prepared in layers for the cool shade of the ride through the city followed by the abrupt heat of the beach.

Here is where they curled their hair, giggling, telling stories, first about boys, then about each other. They dabbed themselves under their arms and applied sweet-smelling lotions. Each bottle made its promises. This elixir would transform the object of its effects into a somehow better person. *"Less frizz is here to stay; be the most attractive you."* As if any of the Health and Wellness girls needed more help in becoming perfectly attractive.

MacKenzie, as had been planned, left the apartment early with Hannah Morgan and Emma Swain. Zora left an hour later, to gather with the other girls at the bus station—where Tina Montclair insisted on squealing every time someone new showed up. Highway 1 that day was awash in winter bloom. Surf vehicles lined the pullouts all the way up to Half Moon Bay.

～

Thumping music and nothing less greeted the young women at the dirt and mudpuddle pullout. The noise was something electronic from Ibiza or Los Cabos. It emanated from within MacKenzie's Mercedes, pelting the Panther Beach parking lot in a hailstorm of sound.

The trunk, *oh, the lovely trunk of the Mercedes;* it billowed with ice and shining pop-top metal; cans of wine in handfuls or more, tequila, rum, piña coladas. Some of the ladies had been drinking already; they teetered noisily across the railroad tracks.

～

The Panther Rock for which the beach had been named sat crouching in its position of the ages, lunging toward the beach and away from the glimmering sea. The tide was low but rising, *bit by bit, wave by wave.* Every so often, a churning rush of white surf pummeled the shoreline, berthing pieces of sandstone and chert from the cliffs, then grinding them back down against the continent once more.

The many sweet fragrances of woman filled the canyon that day. Foldable coolers brimming with ice-cold cans of wine made their way. Beach blankets were spread on the sand by the social committee. Soon bikinis appeared in abundance, and other groups of students from the university (on their own afternoon excursions) began to exchange coyish glances. The winter waves crashed, rumbling, sending their white caps headlong into the tafoni cliffs.

A few of our bikini-clad muses dipped their toes into the sea. Perfect models for youth, and for everything really, they waved to one another and pointed at the rock formations.

Kayla Arroyo was the first to dare venture out. She tip-toed, gingerly dipping and weaving in line with the generous shape of the coast. Soon she had even climbed onto the Panther's back, a far better advertisement than any of the other H&W girls could resist. Turning to see her sisters on the beach below, Kayla Arroyo cheered in triumph.

One by one, each Health and Wellness girl curved her way around the precarious rock formations and onto the Panther's back. It was a marvel to watch: Zora, MacKenzie, Alexandria *Whatshername*—then Emma Swain and Hannah Morgan struggling to lift a soft-sided cooler—one of the type sometimes used in the transport of organ donations.

And there the girls of Health and Wellness stood, sparkling and bedazzled—if not breathing a bit heavily—plump and firm, *awestruck*, as everybody is, by the majesty of the California coast.

MacKenzie stood tall amidst the sea spray. The others gathered around, waiting for her, and only her, to speak. Hannah and Emma pushed through the crowd before slowly maneuvering the cooler into place at MacKenzie's side. The cake inside could no longer be considered fit for public consumption. Emma and Hannah, the bearers of this horrible truth, knocked open the lid of the cooler but did nothing more to reveal its contents to the crowd.

"Weiwei Li was our sister—" began MacKenzie.

Some of the girls cried, but soon enough they thought better of it. No one wanted to smudge their makeup in advance of the photo shoot. First and second tears were blotted with the backs of fingertips then flowed no more.

"And yet Weiwei was so much more than a sister to each of us. She was a model of what every Health and Wellness girl ought to be—fit, involved, diligent in her studies—"

"We love you, Weiwei!" Someone from the crowd was quick to cheer.

"Yes, and this is why we are gathered here at Panther Rock today as our Health and Wellness family—to remember Weiwei the way she would want to be remembered."

MacKenzie nodded, and as she did, Hannah and Emma tipped the cooler, allowing the slump of internal contents to pour out and into the sea.

~

Grave responsibility now dispatched, what followed next was an orgy of photographic delight.

Some of the girls who had been late to arrive ran across the beach. On top of Panther Rock, young women with camera phones swiveled this way and that, completely in line with the time and the place. *Swivel and click, swivel and click* that was the newest dance craze of the twenty-first century. The stragglers then arrived, stooped and leaning to catch their breaths, beige and cream dollops set against the marine sediments of the Northern Pacific.

~

The winds picked up as they would have every afternoon around this time. No bother, out came the floral coverups and tasteful wraparounds so the photo session could continue unabated. Audrey Hepburn and Marilyn Monroe had nothing to improve upon the buff, modern women of Health and Wellness. Hundreds, if not thousands, of Panther Rock portraits taken that afternoon are testaments to this fact.

And while it may be true that the sun plots a lower course across the sky in winter, its intensity in California is no less diminished. Emma Swain was the first to suggest a retreat. She wanted to reapply sunscreen and freshen her drink. Slowly and cautiously, the women of Health and Wellness followed, each working her careful way back down the rock formation.

"Zora Dear," tugged MacKenzie. "Please take one more picture for me—without anyone else here—and now that I have my choice of locations."

MacKenzie stood atop Panther Rock, a perfect vision, full and complete. *Swivel and click, swivel and click,* and that was all...until there was a hollow sound.

The sudden commotion struck the onlookers just as it struck MacKenzie—and just as quickly. It had been a wave, a thirty-foot sneaker wave, and before anyone could react, it dragged MacKenzie away, gurgling.

A collective gasp was issued, then a momentary silence followed by screams.

∼

The senior administration was trademark slow to react. MacKenzie was a legacy and her family were donors, so the decanal leadership was more than cautious in issuing a response.

Members of Health and Wellness were encouraged to take time off from classes and coursework. The need for health and wellness checks across the community was immediately recognized. Individual and group grief sessions were offered in abundance. These were voluntary and confidential, and multiple members of the Health and Wellness house took advantage of their every offering.

Healing spaces were reserved at the Student Union for the next several weeks—these being open to both Health and

Wellness members and to members of the student body at large. Counsellors whose collective, personal identities were sure to match every identity group or combination of identities, were recruited to staff these efforts, so no member of the university community would feel unheard or ill-supported.

~

That night, after the statements had been made and the police had gone home, Zora took a moment to scribble another hasty message to HelpSpace.

Twenty-four

*I*t was drizzling ice in the office park in Philadelphia and Sarita Reddy's cough was worse than usual.

"Here's another one from *Ms. WhatshouldIdowithmylife?*" she sniffled over her shoulder at Ted Nelson. "I thought my response last time was good enough, but I guess not."

Sarita then read:

> *Dear HelpSpace,*
>
> *A few days ago I wrote to say I was alright, and that I was investigating the situation. I thought I was happy. But now things have changed and I am unhappy, maybe even unhappier than I was before. Another one of my friends is dead. It was an accident, but I was right there when it happened and I saw everything. I agree with what everyone says about the situation being heartbreaking. It mostly just makes me think about my own mortality, but this seems selfish so soon after the accident.*

Already my sisters are asking me if I'll fill the seat left vacant on the house board by my deceased suitemate. I can't believe they're asking me that so fast when MacKenzie just died like that.

Somebody needs to talk to the parents and administrators who will surely come with questions—I'm sure that's what they're thinking—they've already asked me to write a few words of remembrance.

"It's always the same with these university girls," said Sarita Reddy. "Every semester we have a few."

∽

That week there were deliveries waiting for Zora at the apartment suite. Each sudden appearance of packages was a source of indistinct embarrassment; she worried what any passersby might think of her receiving such ornate packages at such an unbefitting time.

At the Soldiers' Memorial Services Center seminar the following week, Zora sought to regain a sense of normalcy. Her mind was swimming after another day's worth of visitations and vigil planning. She sat at the back of the lecture hall and at once delved into her fantasy world. She read from works of philosophy, inserting *she* in place of *he*, and *her* in place of *his*. Then she read again, this time replacing *she* with *they* and *her* with *their*.

Krystal Davis swept past the back row. Here is where she would explain the audiovisual setup to the presenter. Now is when she would ask again whether or not there would be any handouts. Zora smiled demurely, then spontaneously wrote in the margins of her notebook:

Detach.

Free yourself.

Stand upright.

After the hour, and once the room had all but emptied, Krystal Davis returned and sat close to Zora in the back row.

"I still owe you a copy of the collected works of the Sage," she began.

"First, I should thank *you* for all the wonderful gifts—"

"Those were only a few tokens to express my interest in your well-being. I hope I guessed your preferences accurately and that you've enjoyed it all."

"Is it *your* interest why I'm being invited to join the Institute?"

"*No, of course not.* You are exactly the type we need to lead the Institute into the next era—for the benefit of all under-represented people."

"And what about the Colonel?"

"What about her?"

"If she and this Sage-person want to recruit me primarily because I'm a minority, then I'm not sure that's entirely right either—"

"You are not only a minority, Zora. You are *the* minority, the exact makeup we've been looking for. According to all of our indicators, you are the most highly functioning example we've ever had the pleasure to encounter. So it's not just that you're *a minority*. Be sure of that. *Be sure of that.* Krystal shuf fled her feet, "You asked how we knew you could manage this and more when others have failed? *That's how.* You've tested more purely than anyone. Why don't you just forget about your worldly cares, Zora, and move in here with us at the Institute to further your career in thought?"

"What about my studies? My degree?"

"What about them?"

"My parents might be upset."

"Why would they be? They love you and want you to be happy."

"Well, they're sure to question if I suddenly quit school to move into a compound by the sea—what would they think?"

"Oh Zora, in a few years you'll graduate and realize not everything's so well-defined. You might as well live comfortably at the beach now while you work through it all. In a few years you'll have written your philosophy and achieved more than you could ever imagine."

"At least now I know you're serious about me moving in," Zora paused for a moment. "But there's another thing

I want to say. The way everyone looks at me here makes me uncomfortable."

"Baby steps, Zora. Baby steps. *All good things come with time*. Better you and your ideas represented here than not, that's how I look at it. *Someday you'll see*. Everyone has to make a decision to settle down sometime; you might as well do it now while you can still derive the maximum possible benefit."

~

The architects of the Soldiers' Memorial Services Center had never intended it to serve as a palace of knowledge. It was no less dingy now than it had been in its decades-long service of dinginess. The tile floor was scuffed from the feet of the shabby furniture; the fluorescent lighting flickered uneasily.

"Dr. Dinkelstein assured me he's going to contact you this week about squash," Krystal nodded to remind Zora.

"Oh, right. I forgot about that," was all Zora could say. "I wasn't sure if he even liked me."

Krystal smiled wryly:

"I can assure you that he does."

Twenty-five

ℛebecca Snyder was an old lady from New Jersey who made Swiss psychoanalyst, Max Ferg's theories on psychological types accessible to hundreds of millions of laymen and women by means of her own, groundbreaking personality type questionnaire.

What is less well-documented, perhaps, is that during the last twenty years of her life, her trust, as administered by her heirs—formed the Institute and furnished it with a source of inextinguishable funding. This was a place for the Snyderians to put into practice the ideas first decoded by Ferg and eventually inscribed in stone at his Effington Tower near Basel.

After the time of Rebecca Snyder's death in 1981, the *Snyder-Ferg Type Indicator* would be administered in every school and workplace, in every country and territory in the world. Psychotherapy for the masses seeped its way into every mealtime conversation. The Institute on the Bluffs by the Sea now boasted the most advanced facilities for breeding human accomplishment, all provided in trust from Rebecca Snyder, and all developed to serve the purpose of her philanthropic aims. It was here *and only here* where—across vast expanses of time—the most fervent wishes of Rebecca Snyder and Max Ferg would at last be realized.

Zora's invitation to squash arrived, at long last, via personal courier. It was accompanied by an invitation for personal limousine service to the Institute at the appointed time.

Twenty-six

Squash is played in a four-walled court. The flooring is divided into a front box and two back boxes, with each back box containing a smaller service box. There is an *out line* at the top of the front wall. It extends to both side walls and all the way down to the back of the court on either side. In addition to the *out line* there is also a *service line*. It is located across the center of the front wall waist-high, but does not extend to the side walls.

∾

"*I'm not usually one for squash,*" said a voice. "But I thought this might be a nice, quiet place for us to get to know one another."

A plain woman entered from a door in the back wall of the opulent court. She was slightly taller than average but otherwise unremarkable. Her appearance was so unremarkable, in fact, that she could have been mistaken for being unattractive. But any statement to this effect would have been unfair, especially since she had the most penetrating emerald eyes.

"I'm so sorry," said Zora. "I was told to expect a Professor Dinkelstein."

"There is no Professor Dinkelstein," said the woman. "Dr. Dinkelstein, *I'm afraid,* is nothing if not an illusion."

"But I don't understand—I met Dr. Dinkelstein last week at *View of the Bluffs—*"

"*That was me.*"

"That can't be—" Zora tried for a moment to insist.

"I'm sorry to have tricked you. I've been watching you for some time now."

"*I met Dr. Dinkelstein and—*"

"Zora, we have access to technologies here at the Institute, the likes of which you have never seen or even heard of. The technological innovations we are licensed to employ are tens of generations beyond what you and others see in consumer markets."

Zora noticed the woman had arrived without squash rackets or a ball.

"Tell me please what all this has to do with me."

"I see very clearly that we won't be able to get anything past you," said the plain woman. "You are very smart indeed, Ms. Weaver." She stepped forward: "Meeting visionaries like you is an added benefit of my affiliation with the Institute. Tell me, have you noticed anything different about the Colonel from you, me, or even Krystal?"

"You mean other than her obvious physical disability?"

"Yes, other than the Colonel's physical disability."

"*I'm*—I'm not sure."

"I will tell you then. The Colonel is not of our type. She does not exhibit an XZOQ or XZIQ or even a TZIQ personality type classification according to the Snyder-Ferg typology. Her personality type is far more common, far more mainstream, though she does submit to the Institute's overarching mission ɑs ɑ pɑrt of locɑl ɑdministrɑtion locɑl. We need ɑll types, you see, even though our recruitment of the rarest personality types— people who have been misrepresented and misunderstood for the longest of human periods—has now become our primary area of focus.

"Our support of these underrepresented personality types and of their proliferation—to bring equity to all person- ality types as required for the sake of balance and global sta- bility—is an idea we stand behind steadfastly. *It's something to believe in.* It's inevitable, and our eventual success will make us great as a people and as a society."

The woman with the piercing, green eyes cleared her throat and continued, "As a matter of fact, the Institute sees added benefit in partnering with the armed forces in our work. Inviting members of the military like the Colonel to serve on our board, and to be involved in our governance mechanisms from the ground up, ensures the continued alignment of our interests with those in the federal government. Military involve- ment also lends a great deal of credibility to our mission—from federal to state-level on down. And for those members of the public who no longer care for the military point of view? *Well,* it keeps those folks away too. That's why I'm always grateful to have members of our armed forces, retired or otherwise, serving on our committees and involved in our most important decisions. The Colonel in particular has shown a knack for attracting new talent and organizing our administration in a way that only she has been able to do. I am especially grateful to the Colonel, in fact, for bringing you here to us."

"You are the Sage, I presume?" Zora asked, now that she was sure of it.

"I am. Usually I don't meet our invitees in person like this—but I have reason to believe that you are special."

"This all sounds *really great*, but I've actually been told I was invited to join the Institute because I'm black."

"Initially, maybe yes. But Zora, we at the Institute are seeking allies—*partners, if you will.*

"We know the historical social structures are bound to fail. There is vast inequity in the distribution of Snyder-Ferg personality types. And across most cultures, the rarest personality types are endangered. This inequity is entirely man-made, I'm afraid.

"Our eventual aim is to balance out the population statistics. Only with more balanced representation from XZOQ's, TZIQ's and other underrepresented personality types—will our global society be able to cope with the complex needs of the future. Only by means of a special, XZOQ vessel like you—or many like you—and a means to power, like the Institute, can we enact the social change that is absolutely essential to begin to redistribute.

"In short, Zora, we recognize the need to expand the benefits of the Institute's most executive memberships to a broader spectrum of the population, and in particular, to members like you, so you can deliver our message of hope for the future of man and womankind."

Zora was not sure what she was hearing. She did her best to buy some time:

"I understand there's a prescribed order to everything, and that it's this order which forms the basis of all things. But my personal connection to the continuum is no more than yours or any other's."

"I can see that *you are* indeed special, Zora. But I'm no fool either. I know a young woman like you doesn't want to stand here, pretending to be interested in squash.

"I've arranged for your first private surfing lesson. You'll find a tailored wetsuit in the locker room. Heladia will meet you at the cabana as soon as you are ready."

And with this and a twinkle in the Sage's emerald eyes, she was gone, disappearing through the back door of the court as if through a mystical fog.

~

The HelpSpace alert appeared as a notification on Sarita Reddy's desktop while Sarita Reddy was already at home packing. An upstart competitor in the wellness application market—one located in its own, non-descript office park outside Akron, Ohio—had offered a marginally better title and an increase in pay. The replacement who sat at Sarita's desk sniffled at the cold he seemed only recently to have acquired.

"This is a follow-up from a university student who's having trouble deciding what to do with her life," he announced loudly. He found this amusing to do given the nature of the requests and the tiny size of the office, but he also hoped to elicit more helpful advice from Ted Nelson, who seemed to have dealt with every type of HelpSpace request imaginable. "She's quite sure now that her way of thinking is not entirely aligned with that of—*What is this? The Institute?* Anyway, she's still concerned about her future and doesn't want to burn any bridges."

The new Sarita Reddy coughed loudly, sending a glistening string of spittle streaming onto his monitor.

∿

Ted Nelson was poorly shaven and ornery. The task of training Ms. Reddy's replacement had fallen largely to him, although he received no credit for this assignment and the extra work went largely unrecognized. The bulk of Sarita's queries would now be routed to him, *if the new guy didn't finish them.* It was stressed at HelpSpace that the regular workload of the team needed to be maintained irrespective of any temporary, personnel-related hiccups.

So *"Just tell her to go fuck off,"* was what Ted Nelson, Jr. suggested to the new Sarita Reddy. Followed by: *"I'm going out to get a cup of coffee."*

Twenty-seven

Rolling, limpid and blue, the surf conditions caused no need for alarm. Heladia was ocean-certified and local—every sinew in her tanned body echoed the contours of the coast. Zora composed little poems in her head. The salt-tinged breeze licked her fingertips as she paddled out on a board borrowed from the cabana. A vast expanse of golden sand swept before the women—and beyond that the national beach and the jetty of inky boulders.

Zora ducked under the swells as she had been instructed. At last, here was an experience the books couldn't offer. She let the crystalline water roll over her—an ankle leash her only tether to the distorted world of men and women above. Here, at the crossroads of happiness and destruction, of joy and hopelessness, of fulfilment and sorrow, waited Zora. If the Upanishads teach that it takes a trick to pass over the sharp edge of a razor, Zora would come down over both sides, enveloping the unconsciousness of being whole.

Heladia was indeed a sparkling coach and Zora was something of a natural. Near the jetty, pelicans swooped their awkward dives into the surf. Zora admired the scenery. Then, suddenly, she took in a taste of the sea—an unexpected gulp of the living water—broth of the Gods—undrinkable to mere mortals and to Zora too. She choked, she cried—*Smash*—another colossal wave broke over Zora. She frog-kicked to the surface, now more determined than ever to get up and *ride*.

～

After the lesson, and once another *sesh* with the amazing Heladia had been set, Zora retired to the locker room. On Highway 1 below, the sounds of the crashing surf vied for dominance with the rattle and hum of sightseeing traffic. Down there, and not too far either, the ancient rhythms of man and nature combined in a mesmerizing symphony. This was *it* in California. *This was what it was all about.* The land where everything is possible *and where nothing is.* Zora loved it like she loved the world. She waited patiently for it all to make sense, knowing full-well from her books this wasn't ever likely to happen.

～

Zora peeled from her wetsuit and checked her phone, and as she read what *surely must have been a mistake* from her HelpSpace alerts, Krystal Davis appeared before her. Zora had been too immersed in her duties as MacKenzie's closest friend and heir apparent, to reciprocate any of Krystal's advances from the previous week. Her position now (half in—*and half out of*—her wetsuit) made communication with Krystal at this juncture difficult to refuse.

"How was Heladia?"

"Oh, she was wonderful. Just like you said she would be."

"Heladia is a nice girl—she lives just up the coast."

"I know—she told me."

"I'll arrange for a tip to be deposited into her account," Krystal angled closer to Zora, touching her gently on the shoulder. "By the way, I was wondering if you'd given any more thought to the idea of moving in with us here while you chair your committee? The Institute is a lovely place to live. We would, of course, considering your status as a student, be willing to provide private transportation to and from the university until that time at which you finish your degree."

"While that is very generous," Zora didn't hesitate: "I'm sure I'm not ready for an arrangement like that."

"Yes, I completely understand. This has all been a bit sudden, I'm sure—and some might consider it unconventional. Fortunately, our annual budget at the Institute does permit some room for unconventionality. I've often, during these past several years, tried to remember what it's like to be somewhere where this isn't necessarily the case—but I must admit, it's now becoming quite difficult to do."

"You see, the idea of that makes me uneasy."

"What does? *Success?* Our mission here is to build on the work of Rebecca Snyder in creating a vision for an equitable society for the good of mankind."

"I'm just not sure that's...*me—*"

Krystal was hurt, confused and disappointed:

"I'm sorry but I must have misunderstood. I thought there was something special, something *electric,* in you—*but maybe I was wrong.*"

"There *was—or—there might have been.*"

"There are times when I have doubted, Zora. Obviously, there are times when I still question. *Yes! There are times when even I still question*—One day when you are old, you may regret your missed opportunities—"

Krystal drew close; she took Zora into her arms.

Zora resisted, sobbing, saying: "I don't want to be here anymore. I think I want to leave."

"*Wonderful,*" Krystal didn't hesitate. "I can explain more in the cove. I realize the Institute as a place or as an idea can be difficult to absorb at first. *We're not perfect.* When you join, some of what we do will need to change."

There was a long silence and Krystal could tell she had made an impression. She felt the time arise to make yet another cautious advance:

"The Sage is having a banquet..."

Twenty-eight

*I*t would be a gross misrepresentation to state that the guests enjoyed the Institute banquets more than did the Sage herself, who unquestionably basked in every minute.

Only every-so-often did the Sage throw one of these gala events. For her they offered the appropriate dose of reverence for the movement combined with pithy entertainment. The banquets were long and entailed opulent refreshment; once one was underway, the Institute was overrun with tipsy, titillated donors and guests.

~

Large-scale events were held in the private cove. They started with a cocktail hour in the late afternoon—this according to somewhat variable timing, depending on the season. If the event were large enough, or depending on the set of guests, sometimes banquets ended only the following morning; though they rarely lasted all the way through to daybreak.

The menu was invariably exotic, audacious or continental, depending on the occasion. Both guests and members alike could be sure their meal would be unforgettable and expensive.

Banquets took place only at the behest of the Sage and there was never any set schedule. Guests were invited simply because the Sage had invited them.

Many guests came solely for a glimpse of the mysterious and all-powerful Sage. Still others were there to get their names into the society pages. No other invitation or honor could better improve one's chances.

Attendees tended not to know one another before arriving; they were there for the excitement or the mystery or because they wanted a free meal. Many were captains of national industry, patrons of the arts, *en vogue* intellectuals. Most hoped they might be considered for even the lowest level of Institute membership. It was *no trouble at all* then, to tailor a new gown or tuxedo, fly across the state or country, and, at the end of a long and magnificent evening, find their way back to Santa Cruz or San Francisco at their own expense. Those normally the masters of men and women found themselves suddenly beholden to the magical powers of the Sage for one evening. Here, the Sage enticed them and bought them at the fire sale price of cold, seasonal soups—of bluefin and Hamachi—of wagyu and small plates of tiramisu.

And, after dessert, once the artisan tea bags and commemorative champagne glasses had already been surreptitiously secreted away in pocketbooks and waistcoats, then arrived the magical moment when the Sage chimed her glass to speak.

~

The Sage spoke for however long she felt appropriate on whatever subject had been the reason for the get-together. The content was dependent on the needs of the Institute, a personal whim of the Sage, or sometimes both. The honoring of a special dignitary, the announcement of a major gift, the introduction of a new initiative—anything was possible with respect to what the witty Sage might touch upon in her exciting remarks.

~

More often than not, the hottest celebrity in Hollywood sat at the head table as the special guest of the Sage. Yet there on this evening, *it just so happened,* between the Sage and the Colonel, the place was set for Zora Weaver. She wore a violet gown with a matching amethyst tiara, both designed precisely for the occasion.

Zora spread her golden napkin overtop of her trembling knees, and, quite unlike any of the Sage's other guests that evening, wondered nervously what to say and do. "I don't think I've ever been a part of something quite like this," she admitted to her left and her right.

"Of course, you haven't," said the Colonel. "Most people haven't. Nothing will benefit the cause of your personal advancement more than your work here at the Institute."

"We're looking for more like you," added the Sage, who had been listening but remained silent until now. "Times are changing. People are changing—"

"Yes," agreed the Colonel definitively. "Zora is going to help us find our way into the future."

~

The evening picked up. The first courses arrived. The mechanical drone of conversation threatened to invade even the most localized of chitchat. To the Sage, this was a sound more precious than even a thousand new XZOQ or XZIQ recruits. She followed the rising and falling of the voices amid the clinking of glass, bobbing her head in concert with the roaring wave.

Twenty-nine

Zora was not accustomed to hobnobbing with the jet set. She had no idea what to say.

The Colonel turned to Krystal Davis and was at once presented with an orange-garnished beverage. She sat upright in her chair as much as she could and took hold of the straw between her lips. Once she had taken her dose of refreshment, she coughed.

"Krystal."

"Yes, Mike."

"More bourbon in that Manhattan."

"Sure thing. Let me just grab the waiter."

The tables in the cove floated in a vast lagoon of sand. There, bobbling atop evening gowns and untucked tuxedoes, swelled faces were filled with porcini risotto and tuna tartare. The din of evening conversation continued to blossom; the time for the host to give her remarks drew imminent.

It was a simple enough thing to do. Once the guests had been sated with food and drink, they were ready to listen with full attention. And the speeches of the Sage were never off-the-cuff remarks: the tell-tale sign of a lazy guru. Her words were crafted with the specific intention of being remembered.

~

Krystal Davis stood and chimed her glass and the resonating waves called to attention guests and donors throughout the cove.

"Distinguished members, invitees, guests. Please join me in welcoming the majestic Sage—"

The Sage brushed her sandy hair back from her eyes. As she did, the cove thundered with enthusiastic applause. The speaker stepped forward a half-step to the table, savoring this moment above all others, as was her habit to do. Then she stood and waited for the applause to die out.

Krystal manipulated the console to control the microphones. No further words of encouragement were required.

"Welcome," the Sage began, "I trust you have found the work of our chefs to your liking and hope that you are availing yourselves to the veritable cornucopia of benefits and wonders on offer here at our Institute by the Sea."

There was a robust round of applause.

"Some of you know me personally. All of you, I trust, have heard something of me—"

A murmur of a giggle rose over the crowd. Once the small, rolling wave had crashed upon the dais at the head of the cove, the Sage continued:

"All of you know me for different reasons, and all of you are here for your own reasons tonight. Whatever those reasons, it is a distinct pleasure for me to welcome you."

A polite applause ensued.

"And no pleasure excites me more than the opportunity to introduce a new force for good in our shared work."

The applause rolled on, gaining momentum.

"And though she is young in years, she has already set a course for change by her involvement and leadership here at the Institute."

The cove thundered openly with support.

"Ladies and gentlemen—directly to my left, may I introduce to you—Miss Zora Weaver."

Krystal Davis, who had once again taken her seat, dabbed at the corner of the Colonel's mouth with a napkin. She gazed around and congratulated herself on another job well done.

All around cove, attendees readied themselves behind brandied espresso and fine, Italian pizzelle. The white linen tablecloths were scraped and squeegeed and readied for the next course.

Courteous applause continued to patter. This patter echoed between the sandstone walls. It grew louder and louder under encouragement from the Sage's flowing gestures. The Sage glanced from her most ardent admirers to the newest guest and collaborator at her side.

But Zora was gone—

⌒

It was one of those perfect West Coast sunsets. On the rock jetty, a handful of figures adjusting waterproof headlamps stood in stark contrast to the glowing horizon.

Zora recited a favorite line from Mariko Nakagawa as she grabbed a board from the cabana. She watched the night surfers push off toward the dripping sun. Then she too paddled out—leaving the crumbling institutions of her previous life behind—to float between the currents and the waves, in search of her one true and most salient identity.

Thirty

*S*ix months later and 7,350 miles away....

Santa Cruz to San Francisco. SFO to Hong Kong. The blurry late-night neon and subpar hostels of Tsim Sha Tsui—jetlag—travel-induced insomnia. Then, once she had gathered herself, Zora hopped a flight to Kunming and another to Gyaitang at the base of the mountains.

Before, the means of transport had been slick and silver and streaming. Zora had travelled the world in days, mere hours, under blankets and atop cushioned seating with trays of delectable meals. The small bus which now delivered her into the mountains seemed of a different, earlier era. It was outfitted in ornaments and bangles, both inside and out—red, green, blue, yellow—all of which made it properly fit for service through the mountain passes and high winds of the Himalaya.

There were no electronic chargers under armrests for personal use; the seats, sometimes without cushions—sometimes without seats altogether—were ventilated by half-windows which sometimes wouldn't open. The passengers, local villagers mostly, clung to plastic bags filled with goods from their long trips into the big city. The ceiling was nestled in a plush, velvet upholstery. Below it hung figurines depicting the Jade Emperor and the Dragon Gods, and even Lord Ganesha. A dim light fought its way into the space, past the drawn shade curtains and bangles and prayer flags.

~

Zora slept across sacks of rice and several books lay scattered in her lap. She dreamt vividly of a destination she had never before considered until now. Two roosters fought in the aisle. The loser, as part of an unplanned retreat, fluttered to within an inch of Zora's ear.

"*Yingle. Yingle,*" announced a man with a wad of cash as he collected the bird, leaving Zora feathered, slightly carsick, and wishing she were still asleep.

~

The bhikkhuni who spoke a little English came back the aisle and sat on a box of bananas. She and Zora said hello in English, then in Mandarin, before holding hands and smiling together deeply. Zora found it was required to shake and even hold hands for inordinate lengths of time with her fellow travelers here, this particularly when the bus stopped for scheduled and unscheduled breaks and mealtimes.

"Your novice?" Zora asked.

"She is not used to the road," the bhikkhuni made a gesture reminding Zora of her own, not entirely subsided, motion sickness. Then the bhikkhuni nodded to an atlas spread across Zora's thighs.

"You learn about Ag-Agra?" She asked without allowing Zora the opportunity to answer. "Ag-Agra is no place to find on a map."

"No, I suppose not."

"Because were it were so simple, Ag-Agra would already be on every map," the woman cackled. "Tell me," she asked, "why do you seek it?"

"I'm not sure that I do."

The woman's eyes rolled back in her head. She nearly fell from the box of bananas.

"*Ah*! I was right then and *it is you* who surely does," the bhikkhuni became very serious. "Let me tell you—if it *were* there for one to find—it would be ice and rock and wind and cold—absolutely not a place for a beautiful young girl and her...*vlogs*." To this the old woman gave a hearty chuckle before asking, "What is it you want from Ag-Agra?"

"I'm searching for the essence of the continuum."

"*To the pure aesthete there is beauty in everything...*"

The bus rounded an especially precarious curve and the old woman was momentarily thrown from her makeshift seat. Once the vessel had righted itself, she asked: "How does a young girl such as you come to seek the continuum? The continuum is something of no interest to most Westerners and especially not to *children*. No—*children* usually aren't interested in the continuum at all."

"There are some people I met in California—"

"*Oooh, California,*" the nun repeated with the largest of eyes.

"Some good friends introduced me to the concept—surfing friends."

"Surfing friends?" The woman seemed to have trouble getting this combination of sounds from her mouth, but Zora inherently understood what she was trying to say.

"They are night surfers, actually. They surf together at night under bright lights. I'd tell you more, but the night surfers don't really like it when people do. They only want to be associated with people who are either really into night surfing, or really into the continuum. Otherwise, they told me, too many *posers* might trouble them with questions that don't really matter."

"Yes, I understand," the bhikkhuni nodded. She wiped a cup without handles and filled it with alcohol from a sack at her side. Her novice, now appeared from down the aisle looking grim, took the cup from her master and drank a long pull. "It will soothe her stomach," the bhikkhuni explained. Then she refilled the cup once more.

∼

There were no empty seats. The driver's wife sat on the stairs at the entrance with a child on each knee. The driver and family provided an air of nomadic domesticity; the frontmost end of the bus was cordoned off for the young things to scramble, for the missus to work on her knitting, and to bubble up stews in a small brazier plugged into the electric cigarette lighter. Here the family whiled away the days and weeks and months, all the while whipping around the bleak, wintry curves of the Himalaya at great and sometimes rattling speed.

"Suppose you *do* find the essence of the undifferentiated aesthetic continuum out there," mused the old bhikkhuni "What are you going to do with it?"

Zora's abilities in Chinese, shaped by three semesters of introductory Mandarin and her mere 72 hours in this foreign country, were suitable just enough for her to inaccurately exchange courtesies about the weather, or to inquire about the general state of someone's health. But they were not at all pliant enough to sustain lengthy conversations.

These words, it so happened, Zora had prepared in advance. She had been reciting them to herself again and again as a sort of personal mantra: 观复万物, 生生不息, 只要我们比肩长行, 就会回到我们来时的地方. *Side by side we walk, the continuum and I. We are one and the same, so I must return to it.*

～

Ag-Agra was indeed the place that wasn't on any map. It was there to be certain, but such thought as to give it a name had only been granted by Garvey Heathcliff, the Englishman who wrote the first best-selling, mass-market paperback, which happened to be set in the place. The Chinese, who act as administrators for the region, have changed the name with varying frequency since then, sometimes with the aim of attracting tourists, and sometimes with the opposite aim of keeping them away.

The bus dropped Zora at the side of the road with animated help from the friendly bhikkhuni. The place was correct, she assured Zora and the driver, or at least as correct as it could be. Then the door closed behind, rattling its chimes as the bus shot like a cannonball still higher up into the mountains. Zora at once set off on foot through the snow.

From behind a boulder, a friendly voice suddenly called out to her in English: "Mind if I walk with you?"

This surprised Zora so much she nearly fell into a snowdrift.

A bearded man wearing a fur hat and wrapped in animal skins stood there, as if sent by divine interruption to greet Zora, either for good purposes or ill. He was a disheveled white man, tall, with a sunburned face where jagged icicles had frozen to his beard.

"I don't know about you, but I'm still not used to this climate," remarked the man. His pants were fashioned from animal hide and his sleeveless jacket had been culled from an until-recently-living, Himalayan yak.

If Zora were to have been murdered, she thought, it must surely have already happened by now. "You can join me if you want," she offered. "Although I freely admit, I have very little idea of where I'm going."

"*You seek where the sun shines on a cliff face in a certain river valley at the perfect time of day under the most ethereal light,*" the man said almost without interest.

Zora stared.

"How did you know I seek the continuum?"

"*You're here, aren't you?*" Laughed the man. "It's *you* who have found *us.*"

"May I ask—" Zora started.

"Ted. It's Ted Nelson."

"*Oh, hi Ted,* and how long have you been here in Ag-Agra?"

"Only about six months."

"Can you take me to experience the continuum, Ted?"

"Yes, we have it here. Come with me. It's quite a hike, but I've found the perfect view."